SCHOOL VENDETTA

JOSHUA M. DOWNEY

Book Cover designed by Joshua Salisbury

ISBN-13: 978-0692149690

Edited by Jessica Prosser and Shannon Wahl

First Edition

10 9 8 7 6 5 4 3 2 1

To Mother, Who once told me, "With all of the great ideas I've given you, I might as well written the damn book myself," She also had seven words for me every day, "Clean up your room, do the dishes," I am yet to do any of those but that's my little secret, Trust me I try, I do all of them in the sink and disregard the ones on the stove and counter I consider the dishes the ones in the sink. Sometimes I put them in the dishwasher and not start it.

ACKNOWLEDGMENTS

When I first started this writing journey in mid November, I wanted to always get constant feedback on my ways of writing and ideas to keep my self-engaged in writing without stopping for a long period time. The first idea to write this book I shared it with a friend of mine named Ethan Remsburg and he said that the idea for it was interesting to think about, so I decided to get more feedback before I started writing because I really wasn't so sure yet, so I went to another friend in Biology class I told her what I told Ethan and she said that it was a great topic to write about, it would bring an extra kink in the writing work nowadays. Her name was Halei Risbon, she has always thought differently about how we see our world, she's the kind of person who would support anything as long as it helped people for the better, the support from them helped make me go through with writing the book. After I got an okay from both of them I started to write the very first chapter of this book to test the waters, I have never written something this long before. In the meantime of writing I also talked to my mentor teacher Thomas Palguta about writing a book of a certain topic at hand, he said it was very very interesting to talk about in a book and gave his feedback and ideas on what to add. I talked to him for nearly forty minutes straight and still had more stuff to talk about even when I needed to get to my next class, I still do it every day he had to deal with me since November when I first started writing this. Whenever I got settled with writing I decided to have a talk with my English Teacher Andrew Ulmer and told him about what it was going to be about and offered him to read chapter one of the book, he never got back to me but I do believe he read it someday. The reason I think he read it was because I had a B for my final in his class and If we had an A we wouldn't have to take it at all, and I never took it even though on my transcript showed 91% which is a high B for my final in his class. I think that was his way of saying my writing was good. Some days when my Mentor teacher would leave for his meetings I would go over to my Biology teacher's mentor room and talk with her sometimes about science and other school related things, she always liked my writing and gave me ideas on how to make my paragraphs less wordy and really said how my book was in person, her names is Nina King, it was her first year teaching at my school and she wanted all of us to pass our keystones, I passed mine in advance. I had a wonderful 8th Period class which was Creative Writing, we wrote stuff and we shared to the class about once or twice a week, I revealed my idea to them and they all thought it was an interesting topic to dive into. To give credit to all that are supporting me and wasting nearly a whole period on myself I'd like to give, Kara Fisher, April Petesch, Christopher Alam, Calla Martin, Ember Showers, Damon Bilbo, Camden Walent, and Hope Sprecher, credit, they all gave me feedback and helped with how to develop characters better and plot changes that would make this book more realistic and true to what we the people see today in our daily lives.

And lastly my 8th-period teacher, Jessica Prosser, who some days couldn't deal with our off topic activities in class, we got off task on the more crazy stuff that you the reader wouldn't even believe, to being my editor for this book and making it make way more sense than what it had beforehand. I do feel bad for Ulmer reading a chapter of my book and having a meltdown over the grammar. They all made this book better than what I had anticipated. Thanks.

1 ELECTION CYCLE

I went to my locker to get my lunch, and then headed down the stairs to meet up with Sean, who was already walking. I got right behind him and hit his shoulder with mine.

"Hey, you finally caught up to me. The traffic is a little slow," Sean said.

"I heard that Ulysses dyed his hair again. I think I heard it is purple?"

"No, I think it is burgundy. You're an idiot – you should realize that there are different colors in the spectrum," Sean chuckled.

"It's not my fault that I have a hard time with colors. Color blindness is a thing, you know."

"I know, but trust me, there is a difference. He is here today, so you are bound to see him," Sean said. "The hallway is just going to get more crowded if we just stand here; we need to make our way to the cafeteria."

We walked side by side down the overly crowded hallway. We finally made it to the cafeteria. Ulysses was nowhere to be seen. He was most likely talking to the Government Teacher, Mr. Mickelson, arguing about the latest political issues. Sean and I sat down near the door to the exit, and waited for him, as patiently as possible. While we waited, I saw the Rossi brothers walk into the cafeteria, speaking to each other in Italian.

"Oh look, the greaser brothers are here today, whispering love poems to each other," Sean laughed.

"Shut up! They're close enough to hear us," I warned.

Leo gave Sean a dirty look, which was seriously threatening, and then continued to talk to his brother. I didn't know what they were talking about, but Sean knew and wasn't saying. I assumed they were out of ear shot, since they got in line to get food.

"You zounderkite! He heard you say that!" I said.

"Zounderkite? What does that even mean?" Sean asked.

"Google it you idiot! You know, I heard they run some kind of secret underground business, like the Mafia."

"You got to be kidding me, those goons? I doubt that," Sean laughed.

"Alright, if they come knocking on your door late at night, expect the worst. You are totally going to be Swiss cheese," I said. "Not that I want you to become cheese, but still, you shouldn't mess with them."

After sitting and waiting for some time, Ulysses finally walked into the cafeteria. We followed after him, and we found some seats. He said nothing and then suddenly turned to face us, giving us a strange look.

"Your new hairstyle looks nice. Uh, it's burgundy, right? It is way better than the typical brown you see around here," I say.

"I wanted to try something different this time. It was either teal, orange, crimson, or burgundy. Since you have orange hair, Pete, I went for burgundy," Ulysses said.

"My hair is ginger, you know, but burgundy looks nice... I like it."

"What took you so long to get down here? We were

waiting for five minutes!" Sean exclaimed.

"I was talking to Mr. Mickelson about the upcoming Administration Election for our school board and the mayor re-election. Since most of us are in the Student School Board, I thought it would be important to know about it. All of the seats are up for grabs, which makes it the biggest election in recent years," Ulysses explained.

"Really? It seems like those seats have been held by the same people forever! I'm guessing that the current members are retiring this year?" I guessed.

"Finally, an election that has more than one seat up," Sean said.

"The local people around town, including Mr. Rossi himself, are running for the board. I believe that Mr. Rossi wants to be the Board Leader, which has the most amount of power in the system," Ulysses said.

"He seems like a very nice person, through and through. But there have been some rumors that his sons are working for some kind of criminal enterprise," I said.

"That's something that we should definitely talk about, but later. It looks like the grease brothers are heading our way. Look natural," Sean said.

Even though I rarely listened to Sean, I decided to act natural like he said. They sat about six seats away from us, but I couldn't understand what they were saying. I ignored them and wanted to continue talking about the school government. It seemed like The Rossi brothers weren't paying any attention, so we continued.

"From what the new running members are saying, they want to get feedback from the students, to better improve their politics. They want to make the district better, especially our high school. We have too many issues that we have to deal with, like the fights, gangs, and other bad stuff that we don't know about," I said.

"If we can get them to agree with the student board on ideas and concepts for our school, I bet you that more students would be happy and violence would decrease. When we go to our next meeting during study hall on Monday, we can talk to the members of the board and see what they think about it," Ulysses offered.

"That seems good, but we should go see Mr. Mickelson about this because if he gives it his okay, we need to reschedule some of the other items we were going to discuss. This seems like a top priority to the both of you," Sean said.

"Then it's official. We'll go see Mr. Mickelson right away," I said.

We all got up and left the cafeteria, making our way down the hallway. When we got to my locker, I put my stuff in and grabbed my binder. After that, I started to go up the stairs to the third floor and walked down the next hallway. Every time I traveled this way, I thought about the very poor placement of the stairways. The only two sets of stairs were on opposite sides of the building – most inconvenient thing ever. On our way, we ran into Hazel, frantically headed to the cafeteria. She was obviously late and trying to get *something* to eat, before they shut down for the day.

"Hey guys, why are you leaving lunch early?" Hazel asked.

"Uh, we're going to see Mr. Mickelson. Looking for some answers about the upcoming school board and mayor election, mostly the board election," I answered.

"Alright, I was just wondering," Hazel said, heading towards the cafeteria.

"Dude, what was that? You were blushing," Sean teased.

"What? No, I was not! Ulysses, did you see me blush,

or is Sean making stuff up again?" I asked.

"Shit, she must have noticed that. Girls don't miss anything. They see the littlest things!" I exclaimed.

"Unfortunately, you can't get with her. She is the girlfriend of none other than Leo Rossi. That guy won't even let you talk to her if he is around," Ulysses said.

"How can some slick back, dark hair, little Italy boy get her as his girlfriend? Like really, you must be joking," Sean said.

"Sean, what did I say about being racist? You are going to get yourself hurt one of these days," I said.

"Dude, you can't argue. He is right in a way, whether you like it or not. That guy had a bad rep," Ulysses added.

"Well, you admitted to liking her, which means that if she finds out, and she probably will, she will tell her boyfriend, and you are screwed. She loves drama, and you know she'll make up a bunch of crap to start stuff, and people will believe it," Sean said.

"You've got to be kidding me," I said.

"Don't do anything stupid, that's all you need to do…simple," Ulysses said.

"Hold up, you are telling this to the person who has

the *worst* luck ever. I've fallen down three flights of stairs, been attacked by dogs, stabbed myself while cooking, and cracked my skull after spinning around in circles...it's going to be hard," I sighed.

"Well, we need to get to Mr. Mickelson's room before the lunch period is over," Sean laughed.

We started down the hallway again, trudging up the last few steps, and went into Mr. Mickelson's room. He was sitting at his desk, engaged in writing something down. We walked towards his desk, and he didn't seem to notice us right away.

"Oh hello, what brings the three of you here?" Mr. Mickelson asked us, as he looked up from his stack of papers.

"We wanted to get more information about the upcoming election that has just started for the school board administration," Ulysses stated.

"Ah, yes. We have just started getting the word out to the community, contacting the local news and posting information through various social media platforms. This election is going to be huge. *All* of the current members are retiring. As of right now, not many people know about it, but later today, you can be sure that our little town of Dutchville will be abuzz. The city council and the mayor are expected to be interviewed, later today.

All prospective members are running individually, with no established party affiliations, so it is going to be very interesting when we vote later next week," Mr. Mickelson explained.

"So, what about us? What can we expect, the student school board, after the new members are elected?" I asked.

"Glad you asked. Since the board is going to be brand new, I'm hoping that I can get the members of this high school, and the middle schools, to work with them. Together, we can offer help and give advice that can make our district better than it was when the old members held power. The older board members pretended that it was still the 1970s when they made decisions for our school. Having fresh people will hopefully mean that they will be more willing to help us," Mr. Mickelson continued.

"You know, I think sounds great too. With the election coming up, I believe that we should call for a student school board meeting on Monday, during first study hall, and open it so that anyone who wants to can attend. What I'm thinking is that we can try and spread the word to others, so that their parents know about how important this is. A meeting now would also be a way for us to recruit new members. Interested candidates could stop by and talk about how they would be beneficial as members of the board and their visions for our school. If you are willing to help us, we can sponsor a debate, open to the public, to help determine the administrative board leader, president, and vice," I said.

"Alright, I talk to the Dr. Chevalier about this. I'll include you on an email to organize the debate, and I don't think that there will be any scheduling conflicts. I look forward to it," Mr. Mickelson said.

Sean chimed in, "It was nice to talk to you, Mr. Mickelson. We can always count on you, for political news and advice."

We all said our goodbyes to Mr. Mickelson and left his room. As we were walking down the hallway, we saw some kids in a small circle. They were cheering, and it looked like the people in the middle were fighting.

"Hey look at this," I said. "It looks like some kids are fighting."

Even though I was afraid that things could get out of

hand, I moved towards the circle.

Sean moved to stop me, "Oh, come on Pete! It's just one fight. It's going to happen anyway. We shouldn't ruin our Friday over something this petty."

"Really Sean, I don't even know what to think about you these days," Ulysses said. "We should get over there quickly and stop them before it gets out of hand."

I dropped my binder to the floor, and as we got even closer, we saw two individuals in a heated argument. It looked like Tom, from Ulysses's English class, and Wilson, from College Algebra.

"Tom! Wilson! What are you idiots arguing about?" Sean demanded.

"This scumbag tried to shove me down the stairs! I almost fell and broke my neck!" Wilson shouted angrily.

"No, I didn't! You are making shit up again!" Tom yelled.

"You guys both need to settle down. There is no reason for this to get out of hand," I said.

"I'm done with this moron," Tom said. He moved to walk away, but then all of a sudden, he turned and ran straight towards Wilson at full speed, tackling him to the ground in a fraction of a second. The group of people started to cheer, like it was some great entertainment to watch other people hurt themselves over dumb things. So, I took action and jumped in, to attempt to stop them from hurting each other. Sean and Ulysses just stood there and watched. *Oh well,* I thought to myself. I just didn't want anybody to get hurt.

Both of the boys were very strong. Tom was a little shorter than me but fierce, and Wilson was almost six feet tall. I grabbed Tom from behind and put him in a chokehold, pulling him back away from Wilson. Ulysses saw what I was doing and stepped in, grabbing Wilson to take him away from the scene. I slowly let go of Tom, who was on the floor, and started to walk away, heading back to the stairway. No teachers ever stepped in to help us, but it was okay. I did it, and that was all that mattered. Wilson walked the other way, and we didn't see him after that for the rest of the day.

"That was awesome, Pete! You did great out there. You really showed them what's what!" exclaimed Sean.

"Well, I only did what I had to do. No one else seemed willing to help stop the fight," I scowled.

Ulysses looked at Pete, as blood started dripping

from my nose.

"Before we do anything else, Pete, we should take you to the Nurse. Your nose is bleeding," Ulysses observed.

"Shit, I can feel it. We need to go before it gets worse. I hope we can get back to class before the bell rings," I say. "I really don't need another tardy."

We made our way to the stairs and down each hall. I had my nose covered to make sure none of the blood dripped on the floor. We finally got to the nurse's office and walked in. I sat down and waited for the nurse to see me.

The nurse took one look at me and ushered me onto a cot. "Just look at you, dear – you're a mess!" nurse Grouse exclaimed. "Let's get some pressure on this."

"Hfss it bwoen?"

"I think it's fine, honey. Now tell me, what happened?" she questioned.

She pulled the gauze away so that I could talk. "I tried to break up a fight. It worked, but I must have gotten punched."

She moved closer to me and felt my nose, proceeding to clean it up and ridding my face of blood.

"Well it definitely isn't broken or anything. You are okay to go back to class now. You got lucky this time, young man. Usually, fights lead to more serious injuries," she said as we walked out.

"Hey, Pete, if you're up to it, why don't we all meet up after school today, so we can continue our election plans?" Sean asked.

"Sure, we can meet at my house. My parents are out of town for a couple of days...they went on vacation without me," I said.

"Jesus Pete, your parents are never home," Ulysses said. "I'll grab Harper on my way."

"Sounds like a plan," Sean said.

We split up to go to our last two classes, to finish off our eventful Friday. Thankfully, I had Geography and German.

2 WALK HOME

Right after eighth period, I hurried out of German class, which was on the third floor, intending to get to my locker, as fast as possible. Sean was on the first floor, and so was Ulysses. Since there wasn't anyone around to yell at me for running down the hallway, I did it. When you can get away with stuff, I tell you, those are the best moments in school. When I got down to the second floor, I saw Hazel with Leo, and they were talking about something. I caught part of their conversation and decided to slow down so that I could listen. Just as I suspected, they were talking about Sean. I felt compelled to stop and say something.

"Hey Leo, don't worry about Sean. He's a racist jerk, and everybody knows it. I don't know why he acts that way, but I'm his friend. Since I know for a fact that he isn't going to apologize in person, I thought I would apologize for him," I said.

"That bratwurst-eating Nazi better not do it again or I'll find a way to get him back and he won't like it," Leo threatened.

Just then, Stefano came up to Leo and started to speak to him in Italian.

"Ehi, fratello, cosa stai facendo con questa testa di carota? È un amico di quel ragazzo tedesco razzista. Non perdere tempo con lui, abbiamo cose migliori da fare. Se sentirai parlare di cose stupide, ci prenderemo cura di lui." *"Hey, brother, what are you doing with this carrot head? He's a friend of that racist German boy. Do not waste time with him; we have better things to do. But if we need to, we'll take care of him."*

I wasn't sure what Stefano was saying, but he didn't look happy. "Guys, I'm sorry. I have to go," I said, turning to go back down the hallway.

I walked away from them and was finally able to get down the remaining flight of stairs, to get to the ground floor. I walked through the crowded hallway and found my way to my locker. I opened the door to get my book bag and started to stuff in my books and binder to take home. There were always some students who lingered in the hallways at the end of the day, talking and texting. I closed my locker door, stood up, and started to walk down the hallway. I passed the office where some teachers and administrators were talking. I kept on going and saw Ulysses walking towards me.

"Looks like you made it through the rest of your day," I said.

"Sure did. I haven't seen Sean though. He must be somewhere around here," Ulysses stated.

"We'll probably have to look for him. You know he gets lost in this giant school of doom. He's probably wandering around on the second floor, looking for a map," I joked. "We should get going before he winds up on the opposite side of the building from us."

We went back to where I came from, to the middle of the hallway, in an effort to look for Sean. The hallways were nearly empty, since it was Friday and everyone wanted to get home. We did a quick search of the second floor and then split up to cover more ground. At a loss, I decided to check the auditorium, but after looking inside, there was no sign of Sean. After that, I walked passed the bathrooms and decide to check them. I swear, the school sometimes has a haunted feeling. All of the other students were gone, and when I went into the bathroom, all of the lights were off. Suddenly, one of the stall doors swung open, hitting me in the face, and causing me to drop to the floor. Sean walked out and looked like he saw some kind of ghost or something; his face was red, like a tomato.

"What the heck, Sean? What are you even doing in the bathroom at this time?" I asked.

"It doesn't even matter. I heard those stupid Italian kids talking, so I decided to hide, to see if I could catch the latest from little Italy," Sean said.

"What were they saying?" I asked.

"They were talking about the student election that is coming up, and they know we are running for reelection. Those assholes want to run again too. They want to make their Blue Party school-wide, to make the school communist, or some shit like that. You know they will do it, and people around here better wise up because those pricks are sick and twisted."

"That is impossible. The school will never, never allow that. Everyone knows that we are going to work to use the upcoming elections to open up communications between the school and the board, to make everything better. It's common knowledge that the Rossi brothers aren't interested in playing nice," I said.

"Yeah, but they know what they're doing, and once someone is elected, it is very hard to get rid of them. And with them in charge, anything they decide to push will become policy," Sean said.

"They will probably make the Blue Party look great to the other students," I said.

"This is going to be some election," Sean said, as he started to walk out.

"So, you were in the bathroom spying on the Rossi brothers, and somehow got lucky enough so that when they walked in, they never noticed that you were there, and started discussing their private lives?" I asked.

"Yeah, so what? What can I say? I'm good," Sean said, smirking.

"Alright, whatever," I shot back. "We should get going. Ulysses and I split up to look for you, so now that I have, we can get going."

Sean and I walked out of the bathroom and started walking down the hallways to find Ulysses, who thankfully, was right around the corner.

"Where were you at this entire time?!?" Ulysses asked.

"He was in the ladies' room, spying on the Italians," I said.

"Interesting...what were they even talking about? You learned Italian just to spite them. Did it pay off?" Ulysses asked, suppressing laughter.

"As a matter of fact, it did. They were talking about running again, in the election against us, expanding their The Blue party, to reestablish a tight grip on school policies, to run everything like the communist pigs they are," Sean returned.

"This is not good. I can see a lot of the students supporting the party because they are afraid of them. With their influence, we stand almost no chance against them. This election is going to be like war. We need to get to your place and make a plan," Ulysses said.

We all started to walk down the hallways again, making our way out of the front of the building. Once we were outside, we saw Harper waiting for us. I decided to fill him in.

"Harper, it has been awhile," I said.

"I know, I'm glad to see you! So, anything interesting happen to you today? My day was pretty chill, which is rare for a Friday," Harper said.

"Dude, you won't even believe what happened! Pete totally broke up a fight, *and* I found out that the Rossi brothers are planning some commie takeover of the school," Sean practically shouted.

"Whoa! That was *way* more interesting than my day! Pete, bad-ass! And the info on the Rossi brothers!?! Sean, you have some balls to risk spying on those guys! Why were you even in there anyway? Kind of creepy," Harper responded.

"I had to piss, man. Besides where I go and what I do is my business," Sean said.

"Guys, let's get going before some crazy teacher yells at us for hanging around the school," Ulysses stated.

"Ulysses is right. Besides, we have to get started on plans for our election. You want to come," I asked.

"Sure. Where are we going?" Harper asked.

"We are going to my place for the weekend. My parents are not in town for the week," I said.

"Really?!? Your parents are never home! Like, what

do you even do when they are never there?" Harper asked.

"I do whatever; it's not that bad. They're not that strict, and I like having my freedom," I said.

"Don't you have a girlfriend? If my parents were gone all the time and I had a girlfriend, she would be over at my place. You should really have her over," Harper added.

"Yeah, she stayed sometimes, but we ended that weeks ago. Anyways, we need to get going," I said

"Oh, okay. You can fill me in on the way," Harper said.

We started down the sidewalk, heading to my place. My house was about six miles from the school so it was a long walk. Even with everything going on, the four of us walked in silence, all in a row. Harper was the tallest out of all of us and was walking fairly quickly. The only time we broke the silence was when one of us would have to tell him to slow down.

I was pissed. I had been keeping my breakup a secret because I knew that my friends would mess with me, especially Sean. It's not like any of them had any girlfriends anyways, so I didn't know why it even mattered.

As we walked through my neighborhood, we saw kids having fun and running around. They seemed happy because it was Friday and most of the kids were pumped about going to the basketball game that night. Personally, I don't like many sports, other than soccer, which Ulysses calls football because he likes to be a hipster. His hairstyle and continually changing color all scream hipster, but he totally denies it. Typical hipster.

"Ugh! I am so sick of walking!" Sean complained. "It feels like we have been walking for hours," he groaned.

"Seriously? We have only been walking for about ten minutes, and you should easily be able to go another twenty before burning out. I'm not tired, and I'm not even as fit as you," I said.

"Fine, I can deal with another twenty, but still, you seriously need to get your license. You're old enough to drive," Sean said.

"So," I shot back, "You are too, and I don't see you getting a learner's permit."

"Nice burn, Pete!" Ulysses laughed.

"Alright, fine, you're right," Sean said, clearly irritated.

We continued on in silence. Another fifteen minutes passed, and we saw Hazel with Leo, at his house, lounging on the front porch. They were clearly talking about something, and it didn't look good. I waved at them, but they didn't seem to see. It didn't look like Leo's parents were home either. An old 1960s looking mustang drove by and pulled into the driveway. It was Stefano, Leo's younger brother. He was definitely the more approachable of the two, but also short tempered, according to Sean. He got out of the car, but I didn't want it to seem like I was staring, so I continued to walk, catching up with my friends, who didn't even seem to notice that I was gone. I hurried to fall in behind them, and they didn't even hear me. It's not like I was being quiet or anything. Of course I didn't see the giant branch on the walk in front of me, and I stumbled into Sean, causing him to momentarily lose his balance.

"Oh Jesus! You scared me! What the hell are you doing?" Sean shouted.

"Sorry. I was looking at the Rossi house, and I saw Leo and Hazel on the front porch. Then I saw Stefano pull into the driveway, and I just kind of dazed off," I said.

"Did it look like anything was up?" Ulysses asked.

"Well, I don't think their parents are home, and I did

see that Stefano was getting out a bag of some sort. I have no idea what was in it, but it looked weird, kinda like a trash bag," I responded.

"I knew it! Sean, you are totally right! They must work for the mafia. The signs are obvious!" Ulysses yelled.

"This is one hundred percent bullshit! Those Chicken Alfredo eaters are not smart enough to run some kind of 1920s business that died with Capone. There's no way!" Sean screamed.

"Here we go again! Enough of your racist crap, Sean! Even though there is a pretty good chance those guys are into some shady stuff, they don't deserve to be disrespected like that! And Ulysses, you should know better!" Harper scolded.

"I'm telling you, they are into some crazy stuff, and everyone knows it. Why not the mafia?" Ulysses asked.

"Guys, just stop, okay? There's no need to argue about what the Rossi brothers may or may not be a part of, but we *do* need to figure out what to do about the election. That's our only way to head off any trouble, in a civilized manner, I might add," I said.

Everyone finally stopped arguing about the stupid mafia and kept walking. This time, I was thankful for the silence. Unfortunately, the Rossi brothers drove past us in their Mustang, with Hazel in the backseat.

"Look at that car – it's wicked!" Sean said. "Too bad it belongs to those losers...sorry, Pete."

At last, we survived the long walk and made it to my house. I reached for the key in my pocket, unlocked the door, and let everyone in. Out of habit, I turned around and locked the door behind me.

"Finally, we made it! That walk forever," Sean said.

The guys settled into the living room and sat down. Everyone was looking at me, expectantly.

"Hey, Pete," Ulysses said, "before we get down to business, we *need* to talk about your love life. Why did you break up with Erin?"

"Nope, no way. I'm not having this conversation," I responded.

"Oh, come on Pete! You know you want to tell us! Seriously, you know you can trust us with anything, right? I mean, especially the juicy details," Sean jabbed.

"Alright, fine. If this is what it takes, then I'll do it."

"Yes!" Harper cheered.

"Just promise me that after this, you'll let it drop, okay? I thought that everything was cool, but then she hit me out of nowhere with this crazy text."

"What did she say?!?" Sean eagerly interjected.

"I'm getting to that, chill. So, like I said, I thought everything was going great, but then she sent me this text, saying that she wasn't into dudes right now. She started texting this insane shit, like I wasn't sensitive enough and that I didn't appreciate her as a woman. It's like she went insane or something. Anyway, that was it. We went our separate ways," I explained.

"Oh man, that's rough. I feel bad for you, for real," Ulysses said.

Sean was doubled over with laughter. Harper shot him a look and whispered, "Don't be an asshole." Sean tried to contain his laughter, but it was too late. I turned away from them, pretending to get some things together for our planning. I knew it was going to be a long evening.

3 THE PLAN

"We need to figure out how we can form a partnership with the new administrative board members, once they get elected into office," I said.

"We should wait until after the official elections because certain adults could gain our trust now, only to backstab us later," Sean said. "Politicians do shady shit these days."

"Hey, where is Rudolph?" Harper asked.

"Was someone supposed to call or text him about this?" Sean asked.

"Crap! Harper, can you get him? I totally forgot to tell him about our meeting. He only lives about ten minutes away from here, and it shouldn't take you very long to get there and get back."

"He lives right across from the Rossi brothers. You know where they live, right?" Ulysses asked.

"Try not to get shot out there," Sean muttered.

I looked over at Sean, letting him know that I was angry, and watched Harper walk out the door. I stood up and took a moment, watching Harper make his way down the sidewalk. It was already getting dark. I closed the blinds and walked back to Sean and Ulysses.

"We should start reviewing school policies that are already in place, looking for areas to change or amend. Then we can move onto anything we might like to add," Ulysses said.

I grabbed the iPad that was sitting on the coffee table and started to search for our school policies. I walked over to Sean and Ulysses, with the tablet in hand, and sat it on the table. I took a seat right beside Ulysses.

"In case of an emergency, all students should avoid the cafeteria as much as possible," Ulysses read aloud.

"Why would that be a part of the safety plan?" Sean questioned. "Isn't that the largest area of the school? Wouldn't everybody be able to safely fit inside?"

"Yeah, but grouping the students together is the last thing we want to do. It may be large enough, but there are really no accessible exits. We would be trapped,"

Ulysses responded.

"That makes sense. More people would definitely get hurt," I agreed. "That got me thinking about other situations and other areas of the school that may need to respond to an emergency, whatever it may be. Hey, did you know that if there was a fire, trapping people on the top floor, they could take the emergency ladder on the top of the building?" Sean asked.

"Since when do we have an emergency ladder on the top of the building?" I asked.

"We've always had it! You've never snuck up there?" Sean asked, incredulously. "If you go to the end of the third floor, there is a door that is unlocked, but it's very hard to open because it's used so little."

I heard a knock on the door and got up to open it. It was Harper, with Rudolph right beside him. Rudolph was also sporting a new hair color, light green.

"What in the world is that?!?" Sean yelled from across the room. "Does your hair do photosynthesis now?"

I tried not to, but I couldn't help laughing. Rudolph walked in, towards the other guys. I followed behind, catching him up.

"Okay, let me get this straight. We are here, focusing on the administrative elections, when we should be worrying about our own campaigns and election? Rudolph asked.

"I know it's a lot, but we really need to be involved in both. Working with the administrative board could really lead to some solidarity between the school and the community. It will be a great move and help us make some real changes for once," I said.

"If that is our goal, to bring the school and community together, then we should also talk about the two candidates running for mayor, since all three are taking place around the same time. Our current mayor, he's a shady character, if you know what I mean," Ulysses said. "What makes it worse is that his opposition, Mr. McCreedy, sounds just as greedy and potentially more underhanded."

This additional consideration silenced the room, until Rudolph asked, "Hey Pete, what happened earlier today to you anyways?"

"There was this fight between Tom and Wilson over some stupid stuff that happened before we got there. Tom threw a punch, so I stepped in to stop them. I did, but I got a bloody nose."

"Whoa! That's amazing! You're always cool like that, Pete. If anyone ever needs help, you're always there, you know?"

"Thanks, Rudolph. Some people think that I just like the attention, so it's good to know you have my back."

"No problem, Pete."

"Okay, back to planning. We have established that this round of elections is going to be huge, new administrative board members, a new mayor, but hopefully, same student reps," I smiled at the others. "I'm confident that we'll get reelected."

"You know, before Harper came and got me, the whole Rossi clan was returning home, and the boys are not the only ones who are plotting a takeover. Their dad, Ottavio, was pissed. He had a flyer, I think it was for the guy running against him for board pres, and while he was talking, he pushed it into Leo's chest. It looked like Leo was making a move to hit his dad or something, but then Stefano stepped in between them," Rudolph revealed.

"Looks like you've taken some spying lesson from Sean," Ulysses said. "At least you didn't turn into a racist too."

"Hey dumbass, it's not racist if it's true. I hate some people more than others, but not without reason," Sean objected.

"Why don't you ever listen?!? You have some serious issues, and one day, you are going to run your mouth off to the wrong person and wind up getting shot," Harper advised. "Even if you think it's true, just keep it to yourself."

"Naw, that's never gonna happen," Sean gawked.

"Keep telling yourself that," I said.

We all moved towards the table to finish up our campaign planning. It was seven o'clock and pitch-black outside. As things came to a close, I walked up my stairs, the others following behind. I went into my room and looked out the window. I looked at the lights from the other homes, and then past them, towards the direction of the school. It was so dark that I couldn't even see the building's outline. I said nothing and just stared out into the distance. Ulysses walked up and stood right beside me, touching my shoulder.

"Makes you wonder what all of those people are up to out there," Ulysses stated. "We should really do something about those Italians and put a stop to them, before they do anything serious."

"Exactly! We should all go now, since we're together. Let's find out exactly what those wop's are up to, see if we can catch them in the act," Sean suggested.

"You three go," I said. "Ulysses, would you mind staying a minute? There is something I want to talk to you about."

I watched as everyone, but Ulysses, walked out of my room. I looked out the window and waited, until I could see the boys below, walking in the direction of the Rossi brothers' home. I walked back and sat at my desk, looking at Ulysses who was just staring at me.

"So, you wanted me to stay behind because...?" Ulysses asked.

"It's dumb to go out and spy on the Mafia. Sean is my friend and everything, but his obsession with the Rossi brothers isn't going to end well," I said.

"So, you let the three of them go out...don't you care if they get caught, or worse, hurt?" Ulysses asked.

"Not really. Don't get me wrong, I don't want anything bad to happen, but those three will never get caught. Us on the other hand, they would be on to us the moment we left here."

"Yeah, you're totally right. I didn't even think about that," Ulysses chuckled. "There is another reason though, why you kept me here instead of going. I know there is."

"I think I'm crazy," I blurted, "for real."

"Seriously?" Ulysses asked. "Why do you think that? I mean, you call yourself that all of the time, and I get it, sometimes, but you were always joking."

I ran out of my room, down the stairs, and into the kitchen, grabbing a folder, as Ulysses followed behind. I opened the folder, revealing its contents on the table.

"My report...from the psychologist I visited a few days ago. Take a look and see it yourself. I'm actually crazy," I said.

As Ulysses read the documents, I grabbed a glass and made my way to the fridge, getting some pomegranate juice.

"Are you kidding?!?" Ulysses yelled. "You have anti-social personality disorder?!? I fucking knew it! You showed all of the signs."

"Language...you are slowly turning into Sean," I said. "Anyways, this isn't good. When people find out, they are just going to think that I'm some kind of serial killer with no heart."

"Being a psychopath...sorry...having this disorder, it really isn't that bad at all. You know, it's just a handful of jerks that make it worse for the rest of us. The fact that you are dealing with all of this and still feel empathy, that makes you better than all of us," Ulysses explained. "You work better under stress too, which is a plus."

"Okay… then, maybe talking to that guy was a good idea after all. Maybe being crazy is a good thing…you are different," I said.

"Exactly," Ulysses said.

I walked away from Ulysses and went to the living room and sat down. By now it was almost eight o'clock, and there was no word from the other guys. Ulysses sat right beside me, a little too close, but I didn't care. No one else was there anyways. Ulysses was looking at his phone, to see if the guys texted him back, and I looked with him. There was nothing new. Either the Rossi brothers were really doing something worth watching, or they were just taking their time to make us freak out. Since we were alone, I thought it was a good time to discuss something else that had been bothering me. "Are we ever going to tell Sean that Rudolph is a Jew?" I asked.

"Probably not. If we told him, the Jew jokes would never end. He'd probably make memes about it too. We should just keep that one to ourselves," Ulysses responded.

"Do you think that Rudolph should tell him? Then we wouldn't have to worry about that anymore," I said. Ulysses went back to his phone, so I decided to drop it.

"How long is it going to take for them to get back? It's not like they live miles away," I said. "Sean even took my notebook, so I can't even do anything productive."

"And how does Sean even know what they're saying to each other? It seems weird that he hates Italians so much but knows how to speak their language," Ulysses said.

"You are going to have to ask him about that because I truly have no idea. He never gave me the history on that, but I think it was because of some babysitter or something."

After I said that, we both started laughing, hysterically. Then we just sat there, right beside each other. Ulysses felt cold, as if he was dead, and I got the eerie feeling that he was a ghost. The house was abnormally quiet, and there was no sound from the cool, fall air. Ulysses gave me a strange look and then looked away. I started to get up from the couch, to see if the guys were on their way back, but then Ulysses put his hand on my shoulder, persuading me to sit back down. Then he looked at me, directly in the eyes.

"What are you doing?" Ulysses asked.

"I wanted to see if the guys were on their way back. It's getting late, and I am starting to get a little worried," I explained.

"Just sit...please? They will be back sooner than later," Ulysses said. "Looking at you...I mean, you're just...I find you interesting, that's all."

"I don't know why. It's not like I'm special or something. I'm just...me," I said.

"No, that's not true. You are not normal. You are special...you could make a great leader. With all of your abilities...how could people not love you?"

"You know, you are one strange person, if I do say so myself," I said.

"No one is really normal these days, trust me. I have issues too, you know? And some people...wouldn't understand it," Ulysses said.

"What kind of issues?" I asked.

"They're not big issues...it's just that I can be strange sometimes, little things...you wouldn't notice," he said.

"Alrighty then, Mr. Weirdo," I said, pushing his shoulder away from mine.

"Whatever," Ulysses said, fixing himself.

"Hey, why did you dye your hair burgundy? You know, you should just stick with your natural color. It's a lot nicer...more realistic," I said to him.

"I don't want to be just another face in the crowd. Like you, you stand out. You have this great, ginger hair, different from what I see every day," Ulysses responded.

We just sat there, and I could feel Ulysses looking at me. My face started to turn slightly red.

"I don't know why you think that. There is nothing here to like," I said.

We continued to sit in silence and waited. It wasn't very long before the door flew open, with Rudolph coming in first. The guys looked spooked, as if they saw a ghost of something.

"We have a huge problem! We aren't safe!" Rudolph shouted.

"Now what?" I asked, as I turned to face him.

4 DAS STADTCAFE

I jumped off the couch and made my way to the other three, and Ulysses followed suit, walking around instead of jumping.

"What happened out there?" I asked. "Why did it take you so long?!? They only live about four minutes away!"

"We saw weapons in their rooms and a shit-ton of Blue Party propaganda," Sean said. "They are definitely planning something – I told you we couldn't trust those assholes!"

Everyone's faces ran white and cold as Sean said that. I just stood there, not knowing what it all really meant. I was telling myself, They just saw some stupid flyer's and hunting gear, that's all. It wasn't making any sense.

"What do you even mean, they had guns?" I asked. "Probably a bunch of hunting crap, so what? What if they were just looking at them?"

"Are you serious?!? They have guns! They could kill people! Do you think this is some kind of joke?! Do you?!" Rudolph shouted.

"That's what you think they are going to do, shoot people?" I laughed. "Get real; they are not going to do that, not over an election."

"I don't know. I don't know what to think," Harper said. "Just in case, we need to be vigilant."

"You too Harper? You're buying into this? You've got to be kidding me! It's nothing! They are not going to hurt us over something so petty," I said to him.

"You guys do whatever you want. They're going to rig the election anyway, so what does it even matter? Those guns are probably just for show. They're going to use them to scare people," Ulysses commented.

"You guys better wake up! Who cares about the election, now?!? They have way more serious plans, and if they find out we were spying on them, I guarantee we'll be first on their hit list!" Sean said. "We need to figure out a way to get them, before they get us!"

"You're totally overreacting, Sean," I said. "There is no way they saw you."

"No, he's right. I think Leo saw me," Rudolph said. "I was looking in the window, and he looked right at me. It looked like he was going to come outside, so we ran back."

"You freaking idiot! I told you to be careful, not to attract attention to yourselves," I said.

"So, now we definitely can't do anything or tell anyone. If we do, the Rossi brothers won't lose any time coming after us," Ulysses said to everyone.

"Now what?" Rudolph asked. "It's getting late...what are we supposed to do? I know I'm not going back out there for the rest of the night; we could get shot!"

"Everybody, just calm down. We're all freaked out – just stay here for the weekend. Let's get a good night's sleep and figure this out in the morning," I suggested.

I walked back upstairs and went into the closet, to grab some blankets for the rest of them. I decided to sleep downstairs on the couch, and I let the others figure out where they wanted to sleep.

"Okay, two of you can sleep in my room, and the

other two can stay in the guest bedroom. Just make sure you pick up after yourselves."

"Ulysses and I will take your room for the night," Rudolph said.

"Looks like we're getting the guest bedroom, Sean," Harper added.

Everyone started to make their way upstairs, as I made myself comfortable on the couch. It didn't take long for me to close my eyes.

I woke up on the floor, with my blanket over me. I stood up and made my way to the kitchen, to get a glass of water. I opened the cabinet and grabbed a glass, then walked to the sink. After I filled the glass of water, I walked back to the couch to fold up my blanket. I looked at the clock; it said 8:27. I figured I should wake the others, before it got too late.

I walked upstairs and into the guest bedroom, to wake up Sean and Harper. I tapped Harper's shoulder and told him to get up and wake up Sean. I left the room and went into my room, where Ulysses and Rudolph were sleeping. When I walked in I saw them both in my bed, I wondered how they managed to fit. The fact that they were both in there together bothered me, and so without even thinking, I walked closer and dumped the entire glass of water on them.

"Dude, what the fuck is wrong with you?" Rudolph shouted, as he got out of my bed.

"The opportunity was right there, so I had to take it," I chuckled. "It felt great to do that, by the way."

"Not cool," Ulysses said. "But, it's water in the end."

"Just get yourselves together...and put a shirt on, Ulysses," I said, as I walked down the steps.

I put my shoes on and paced around the bottom floor. I decided to go down to the basement, to see if there were any clothes that needed to be washed. My unobservant self didn't notice Sean, walking down the stairs behind me. He got so close that I could feel his breath on the back of my neck.

"What are you doing down here?" I asked, startled.

"I was just wondering what you were doing...you left the door open," Sean responded.

I walked over to the other side of the basement to grab a basket, and Sean followed, about six feet away.

"You came down here for what reason? Are the others ready or something?" I questioned.

"Are you okay?" Sean asked, watching me closely. "You were acting strange last night. Did something happen when you were alone with Ulysses?"

"No, I'm fine. Nothing happened last night…we just sat and talked while you were gone," I responded. "What is it to you anyway?"

Sean didn't say anything for a moment and just stared at me. "Are you sure?" Sean asked, coming a little closer, "When we came in and you looked at us, it felt like we were interrupting something. Is there something going on that I should know about, something Ulysses is hiding?" Sean asked.

"No, I told you. Everything's fine."

I finished filling the washer and turned to walk up the stairs, with Sean following, and we put on our jackets. Then we called the others to hurry up, so that we could leave. I opened the door and felt the cool fall air hit me, as I started to walk out. I knew for a fact that I forgot to shave because when I touched my face, I could feel it. Sean was the first one out of the door, followed by Ulysses then Rudolph. Harper closed the door behind him, and we started to walk down the sidewalk.

"Seriously? You're wearing my shorts?" I said to Ulysses.

"Yeah, why not? They fit perfectly," Ulysses winked back

"Fine, whatever," I replied. "You know you're going to be cold."

Ulysses didn't say anything and just smiled.

"So, where are we going? It is early, cold, and I wouldn't be surprised if the Rossi brothers come looking for us," said Sean.

"There is this good German café about a mile away, and they open at nine," I said. "I've never seen the Rossi brothers there. It's quiet...we can talk more about what happened."

"Sean, is it possible for you to behave when we are there? It's a public place after all," Ulysses commented. "You have to exercise some self-control."

"Do you really doubt me? I have perfect self-control," bickered Sean.

"I hope you know that lying is a sin," Rudolph said.

Sean gave Rudolph a dirty look, and the rest of us started to laugh as we continued our walk to the café. We crossed the street and rounded the corner. At the end of another corner was Café Julia. I opened the door to let everyone in.

"Hallo! Willkommen im Cafe. Wie geht es dir?" Julia said. "Hello! Welcome to the café. How are you?

"Danke vielmals. Wir Kamen Einfach vorbei, um

etwas zu trinken und zu reden," Sean replied. "Thanks a lot. We just stopped by to have a drink and talk.

"Take a seat everyone, and I'll take your order shortly," Julia said.

Sean is good with German; he knows it all too well. We walked to the nearest table and took our seats near a large window, looking out on the now busy street.

"You show off," Rudolph snarled. "Just because you can speak German and Italian doesn't make you special."

"Just get over it," Harper said.

"Cut it out. Julia is walking over," Ulysses said.

"Alright, what may I get you five gentlemen?" Julia asked.

"Ich werde den sechzehn Unzen Kaffee haben, der mit drei Esslöffeln Zucker und mit Milch entkoffeiniert ist," Sean answered. *I'll have the sixteen ounces of coffee decaffeinated with three tablespoons of sugar and milk.*

I wanted to show Sean that I could speak German too, so I ordered, "Ich werde den schwarzen Tee mit einem halben Esslöffel Zucker und ohne Milch trinken. Stellen Sie sicher, dass es nicht kochend heiß ist." *I'll drink the black tea with half a tablespoon of sugar and no milk. Make sure it's not boiling hot.*

"I'll have the regular coffee with no sugar or milk in it," Ulysses said.

"I'll get the English breakfast tea with four teaspoons of sugar and no milk," Harper said.

"I'll get the same thing as him," Rudolph said.

"Danke," Julia said as she walked away.

"The both of you are such show-offs," Harper said.

"Sean started, and I followed," I said. "And so what? I can speak it too, and if I don't want to lose it, I might as well take advantage of opportunities when they present themselves."

"Speaking of languages, Sean, how do you know Italian so well, when you don't even like them at all?" Rudolph asked.

"Yeah, we all want to know," Harper said.

Sean sat up in the chair and started to get his phone out.

"See, it began when I was young. I had this babysitter who was from Italian descent. She spoke English very well, and she offered to teach me Italian. Of course I said yes, and for two years, she taught me as much as she could," Sean explained.

"Very interesting, Sean, but can we finally talk about

your little spy mission last night," Ulysses asked.

"Alright, this is what basically happened. We left the house, as you know, and made our way to the Rossi's. Once we got there, they had the lights on, so we started to move closer, to see what they were doing. Being the tallest one here, Harper looked through the window. He saw Leo walking down the hallway with that Colt switchblade of his, in his hands. We all crouched down and snuck over to the other side of the house, where I saw Tom, Leo, Stefano, and James talking around a table. They were talking about the upcoming election. At first, it seemed harmless...they were just talking about school stuff. Then Stefano walked over to a closet and grabbed the black bag you saw earlier, along with a lot of printed material, related to the election. When I saw that, I moved to the other side, but made a loud enough sound that they knew something was outside. That's when we made a break for it back to your place. I don't think they knew it was us," Rudolph explained.

"What about the guns?" I asked.

"Serious stuff...the only thing I could identify was a M1911," Rudolph said.

"You are telling me that Leo had a M1911 in his

hands?!?" I exclaimed.

"Yes, he did. The gun was grey and had a brown grip," Rudolph said. "To be honest, it looked really nice, but it scared the crap out of me."

"If you don't think that they're in league with the mafia now, then you're all stupid...or blind," Sean said.

"Why is it, that you always jump to such radical conclusions?" I almost shouted. "Okay, I agree that what you saw was definitely shady, but making up crap about the mafia isn't going to do anything but freak people out."

Nobody said anything. Harper was the first to break the silence, changing the subject. "So, what did the two of you do while we were gone?" he asked.

"We really didn't do anything while you were gone," Ulysses said, as he lightly bumped me with his shoulder.

Sean sat there, staring, and then shot a look in Rudolph's direction.

"In a playful mood?" Sean asked.

"Maybe," Ulysses said, smiling. "What's wrong with that?"

"Oh, nothing, nothing at all," Rudolph said.

"Good," I said, staring back.

Ten minutes had passed, and by then Julia came out with our drinks and left us the bill. Being the nice human being I am, I was going to pay the bill. Once we finished, I went up to the register and paid the bill, giving her a tip for her friendly service. After that, everyone got up, and we headed back to my place again, to do whatever for the rest of the day. After we got back, we decided to go to the store and get supplies for our own election.

—

"Where are we going to go to get supplies?" Sean asked.

"We should make a list on what we need so we don't waste money on stuff that is unnecessary," I said.

"We could get markers, larger poster things, and tape to hold it together, when we finish it I can take it home with me and I'll head in early as always to put them up before you guys get to school," Ulysses said.

"We can go the store that is nearby, It has all of the basics for the things you guys need," Rudolph said.

"Okay, let's go then," Sean said.

We leave my house and walk back into town with our list of things we needed for our re-election.

"It would be a lot better if one of us drove instead of walking everywhere," Harper complained.

"It's not that bad, walking is good for you, ancient humans had to walk everywhere to get places, so why do we do it?" I said.

"I mean...It's a long walk to get there, but we are going to have to walk," Sean said. "No other option."

"Stop complaining its one trip to get stuff we need, we won't have to travel this far if we don't anymore," Ulysses said.

"It's for something important just deal with it I see," Harper said.

"You know for a November and it starting to get cold I'm surprised you don't have yourself a red nose for being so pale," Sean said.

"My nose only gets red when I get punched or when it's freezing out, you obviously don't listen to the news because the sound waves must go over you," Rudolph said.

"It's not even cold," Harper said. "You're always full of shit Sean."

"Why is that?" Sean asked.

"You have brown eyes, telltale sign," Harper said.

Ulysses and Rudolph started to laugh and I kept

walking trying not to laugh at was going on but it was hard.

"You shouldn't make fun of him all in one day, he's human to remember? Like the rest of us here...also we are almost here to the store," I said.

"Thanks, Pete, I can take a lot of stuff," Sean said.

We get into the store, the store is called, The Rolling Gnome, strange name, they don't sell any gardening stuff at all.

"Good morning to the five of you, what are you looking for?" the man said.

"Oh hello there, we are just looking around for some poster and markers, we have a school election coming up soon and we need to start campaigning before then," Ulysses explained.

"Take a look around we have the basics in here. The paper and writing utensils are at the back of the store to the left," he explained.

"Thanks," I said.

"Do you think it's a little weird that there is five of us walking around town?" Sean asked.

"It's strange but, I don't know why you would think traveling in a group is weird, safety in numbers is the best," Harper said.

"What's the best color for the posters?" Ulysses asked.

"We can do pink, purple, and maybe red, to be an eye catcher," I said.

"Purple? Why have that ugly color," Sean said.

"To appeal to the female students, since you ruined it over the last year," Ulysses said.

"What? Oh, never mind. I knew what you were talking about," Sean said.

"Look I'm just saying that if you call a woman the lowest levels of human, don't expect to leave the room fine," Ulysses.

"She didn't even get suspended for it, I did," Sean said.

"Maybe because she's the *counselor*," Rudolph said.

"But still, she was a bitch anyways," Sean said.

"Let's just get the stuff we need and get a move on, we don't have all day to stay in a store arguing about people," Harper said.

We got the poster paper and marker then we left the store, on our way home we people at the town square gathered up, must be a candidate doing some kind of speech.

"We have better things to do than listen to a speech," Ulysses said.

With the temperate weather continuing we make it

back to my house and start setting up.

"Make sure you get to school early Monday before we even make it, I want to see it before I get in so I can give you my opinions as if I was a walking into the school student," I told Ulysses.

"Will do, I'll get Mickelson to take a look as well before you get in," Ulysses said.

5 THE CAMPAIGN

I got out of bed and got myself together for school. Monday is the worst day in the entire week. From party hard Sunday, to work on Monday. Once I got done getting dressed and brushed my teeth, I got all of my books and my binder ready for the day, putting it all in my book bag. I opened my door and headed out for the day. I turned left to make my way to school, which usually took me about twenty minutes. I left early enough so that I was able to take my time. As I was walking, I saw Sean leave his house and cross the street, meeting me on my side.

"Good morning! I gave Ulysses all of the campaigning stuff for this week's election. He's already in the school setting it up," Sean said. "By the time we get there, the posters and our student table should be set up, hopefully getting across how important this is."

"That's great news, but hey, we are about to pass Rudolph's home, and you know who's home also," I said.

"Those little..."

"Shut the up, Sean!"

"Seriously, I was going to say something nice," Sean said.

"Lies, and I know it. You can't disagree," I said.

We passed Rudolph's house and by the looks of things, he was getting ready to come out to meet us. We got about ten feet away from his house, when he started to walk out, catching up with us, fast.

"Good morning you two."

"You were quick to get out of your house. I hope we didn't rush you," I said. "Sean said that by the time we get to school, Ulysses will have all of the campaign stuff up and ready."

"Speaking of school, you know Ms. Ray, the College

Algebra teacher that Pete and I have for period two?" Sean asked.

"What about her?" Rudolph asked.

"She's hot," Sean said, chuckling.

"Dude, she's a teacher," I said.

"Oh, come on! Just look at her! If you just look at her for a couple of seconds, when she isn't looking, you will see what I see in her," Sean explained.

"You are one sick minded person to think about that. She is like twenty-nine years old for god's sake," Rudolph said.

By the time our conversation had turned to Ms. Ray, we were almost at school, and we were early. I walked into the school and down the hallway, past the office where the office staff looked extra busy. It seemed like they were getting in on election activities as well. Down the hallway, I made my way upstairs to get to my locker, while everyone else went to theirs. There were not many students in the hallways, since we were more than ten minutes early and beat all of the buses. I got my stuff out of my book bag and other things out of my locker, then headed downstairs again to meet up with the others. Sean was on his phone and leaning on the wall, waiting for me, along with

Rudolph.

"Okay, I'm ready to go see the progress on the posters in the second hallway," I said.

"Well then, let's get a move on," Sean said, as he walked in front.

"You know this election is going to be intense, with the whole mafia thing...what if they do something violent or try to turn the other students against us?" Rudolph asked.

"Seriously, Rudolph? I thought we all agreed that what happened over the weekend was just a big misunderstanding?"

"Maybe you did, but the rest of us know what's up."

Frustrated, I attempted to refocus the conversation, "I should start working on my speech topics and a vision for the future of this school, some policy outlines too."

We walked down the other side of the hallway and down the final flight of stairs. Once we got to the bottom, we saw a group of students around Ulysses and Harper, and by the looks of it, they were answering some questions.

"Look everyone, just listen, and we can answer your important questions. Make sure you come to the open forum later, so you can hear speeches on policy and school reform," Ulysses yelled over the loud crowd.

"Excuse me, I need to get up here. Looks like we are actually more popular than I thought were going to be," I said, as I pushed people to the side.

"Okay, everyone should go to class. The bell is about to ring, and we will be having a meeting during first study hall and into the lunch period," Mr. Mickelson said.

"Thanks, Mr. Mickelson. I guess I'll see you during the meeting then?" Rudolph asked.

"Yes, you will," Mr. Mickelson responded. "I need to plan the order of speakers and get ballots ready. The election is going to be this week on Friday, so all of you need to fight hard to win."

Mr. Mickelson started to walk away. I turned to see Leo and Stefano walking down the hallway, with three other people, Tom, James, and Hazel.

"Looks who's here, the dirty Jew and the orange one. I haven't seen you guys in a few days," Leo said, as he was getting closer.

"Well, no shit Sherlock. We just had off for the weekend," Rudolph snarled.

Leo walked up to Rudolph, grabbing his shoulder and pushing him. "Listen here Reindeer! Don't act smart around me, or I'll take you out myself," Leo threatened.

"Enough Leo!" I ordered.

"This isn't over," Leo muttered, as he walked away.

"We need to get to Physics, and you should get to class too. And don't do anything stupid," I said, as I walked away from the group.

"I stood there like an idiot and didn't even react when he grabbed me," Rudolph said, following me down the hall.

"It's okay. Sometimes it's better not to. My advice, don't fight unless you have to," I said.

We continued our walk until we got to Mr. Cannon, the crazy Physics teacher everyone in eleventh grade loved. We follow the line to get into his room, and I took my seat, waiting patiently until he walked in. I got out a piece of paper and grabbed a pencil, putting it in my left hand to write the date. Mr. Cannon walked into the classroom after were all seated and waited for three minutes. He was notorious for being late every day. He opened his laptop to do attendance.

"Alright, with attendance complete, we can begin class," Mr. Cannon announced. "Today we are going to learn about the study of light rays and how they affect us."

We sat in that class for forty minutes, learning all types of rays, from radio to gamma.

"We can only see visible light. Gamma rays are the most dangerous rays to come in contact with. That should serve as a lesson to us all that nuclear power should be taken seriously."

Mr. Cannon finished his lecture but stopped me before I walked out.

"I hear that this election is going to be huge?"

"Yes, all of the members of the board are retiring, so they need to fill in the seats quickly before the end of this month. We are also fighting to keep our seats on the student board," I said.

"Good luck to all! I guess with all of the changes, there should be a big turnout at the polls this year," Mr. Cannon said as I walked out of the room.

"Ready for some College Algebra?" Sean asked.

"I guess," I said. "Not as eager as you are though."

I started to walk with Sean upstairs, to get to Ms. Ray's room. The stairs felt really crowed, as if it was New York City. Once we got up there, I started to walk ahead of Sean and into her room, but she wasn't in yet. I figured she must be in the other room across the hall because the teacher in there was talking to someone. I took my seat, and Sean sat right beside me, along with Wilson. Ms. Ray walked in and stood in front of the class.

"Good Monday morning to everyone. Let us continue factoring and using quadratics," Ms. Ray said.

I grabbed the papers from my binder, and we started to complete the rest of the work from Friday. As a group we were almost done anyways, but we decided to go slow and look busy. That way we could discuss other matters.

"For seventeen, did you ever find out what the y-intercept was?" Wilson asked. "I couldn't find it by normal means of calculating."

"Oh, the y-intercept is negative zero, right here," Sean said.

"Negative, zero...you drunk or something?" I asked.

"I wish...I meant negative eight," Sean said.

"What an idiot," Wilson said.

"People make mistakes all of the time; that makes us human," I said. "Anyways, we are almost done, which is good."

We got done with our work and told Ms. Ray that we were finished, and she gave us another paper to do.

Algebra isn't hard, its just that it's annoying when you repeat yourself six hundred times. We started to work on the other paper as a group. It was longer than the first one we did.

"Did I ever tell you, Wilson, that Ms. Ray is hot?"

"No, but I can see it," Wilson says.

"You guys are sickos," I said. "We need to hurry up and finish this. The class period is almost over."

We only got halfway done with the second worksheet before we had to go. I had to go to health, and Ulysses was planning on meeting me there before we went in. I said goodbye to Sean and Wilson as I headed to the ground floor for class. It was one of the most boring classes in school...the teacher pretty much talked all period, as we did our work. Once I got down to the ground floor, I saw Ulysses near the room, looking at a poster from the other political party.

"Hey, ready for health class?" I asked, standing beside Ulysses.

"Sure. We are just going to work on a paper, and I heard she isn't here today," Ulysses responded.

"Thank god! We finally can do whatever we want," I said.

We walked in and took our seats. The classroom was

organized into simple rows of tables and chairs. Ulysses sat right beside me and Leo sat two seats away from us. His brother was in math class with Rudolph.

"Rudolph told me in the hallway that Leo attacked him, and you just sat there and watched," Ulysses said.

"I didn't hit him or anything. There was no point, and I didn't want to cause a bigger scene than there was already. I told him to back off, and he walked away," I said.

"Oh, okay then, *anyways*, our debate is during the next study hall, and it will probably run into first lunch. So, after this, we need to find the others before we head down there," Ulysses said.

"Okay. It won't be that hard to find them, since their study hall is on the bottom floor where the debate is going to take place," I said. "Hey, do you see that? Leo is staring at us in a suspicious manner."

"Just ignore him. He doesn't have an issue with us," Ulysses said.

The health substitute wanted the class to be quiet for the entire period, so it was even more boring than usual. The class took forever to end, but once it did, I left the room as quick as possible with Ulysses, and we started to make our journey to the auditorium where the debate was going to happen. A path cleared for us in the hallway, allowing us to get there faster.

"Here we go…our first debate for the election," I said.

"Luck is going to be on our side – I can feel it," Ulysses said. "I can see the other guys already sitting at the table, waiting for us."

I walked in, "Are we ready for the debate?" I asked.

"We were waiting for the two of you to begin," Sean said.

We took our seats. Mine was in the middle of everyone because I was going to be the board leader, and we waited, as the Blue party members started to walk in.

6 DROPPING DIMES

Sitting in the front of the auditorium, we were facing a crowd of people who were going to watch us speak. Since I was running to remain the board leader, I had to wait until the other students on the board took their seats before I could begin. Some of the Blue Party members, Tom and James, started to take their seats as well. Leo and Stefano had yet to arrive. The crowd began to settle. Leo and Stefano were the last people to walk in. They got up on the stage and sat in their designated seats. Four out of the six seats were held by Blue Party members, and the rest were Red Party, which made it hard for anything to pass as policy. Two of our members, Ulysses and Sean, were designated as liaisons, and they were responsible for working with the opposing party, to ensure that things would work out smoothly. The only real reason the Blue Party had so much power was because of the Rossi brothers; they exercised a lot of influence over the school.

"Since we are all here, I will call for the meeting of the board to begin," Mr. Mickelson announced.

"The first order of business deals with events policy changes. This policy is up for a repeal and replacements, including a plan which will allow students to eat and study outside," I said.

"Considering the current school climate, I will vote *No,* and advocate to keep the current policy," Tom said.

"I will also vote *No,*" James said.

"I am also in agreement, the current policy is fine and should remain," Jack said.

"I am voting *Yes;* change it," Leo said.

"Agree…repeal," Stefano said.

"Repeal and replace it; this is important for everyone," Adam said.

"There is a tie. Pete, it will be up to you, repeal or keep," Sean said.

"With this policy on the verge of changing, I believe

this vote will be the most important. Today, with our schools combating violence and gang actives, it is important to ensure the safety of all. I say repeal and replace. It will make students happier and be a way to provide more freedom," I said.

Some people from the audience started to clap and cheer, indicating their desire for the policy to be removed.

"Now the executives will vote if they want the policy to stay or change," Mr. Mickelson said.

"Both parties have discussed this matter at length, and ultimately, we have both agreed to pass the policy and have it removed from the books. If current members of this council remain in place, after voting, the old policy will be removed. Changes will be implemented as soon as next Monday. Thank you for your support, and we'll see you at the polls," Ulysses stated.

"The next order of business is the upcoming School Board election for the city. Those members of the community, running on the ballot, will now have the floor," I announced. "They will share their ideology on how they plan to partner with our school and the community."

"Today I would like to present one of the candidates, Mr. Rossi, who is a well-established businessman in the downtown area. Please welcome him and listen carefully to what he has to say," Mr. Mickelson announced.

Mr. Rossi walked up to the podium and adjusted the mic in the direction of his face. He smoothed his tie and cleared his throat before he began talking.

"Welcome all. I am Mr. Rossi, one of the candidates for the upcoming election. I am pleased to be here today, to see all who could attend the meeting," Mr. Rossi announced.

"Today is very a special day. I am happy to announce that with the retirement of the current board members, I will start to unveil my policy visions for the upcoming year. The very first thing I want to do is give power back to the students who go to this high school. Previous board members worked hard every day but achieved basically nothing since the 1960s, when the council started putting restrictions on student school board members," Mr. Rossi said.

As Mr. Rossi talked about his policy ideas, I needed to use the restroom. So, I got up from my seat and made my way backstage to use the bathroom, so I wouldn't disturb the others. I made a sharp left and walked down the hallway to the men's bathroom. Once I got done doing my business, I heard someone open the door to the bathroom. Thinking it would be just another random male, I disregarded it and slowly walked over to the sink, to wash my hands.

"Hey, can I talk to you? It's really important," a feminine voice said. As I turned to face the speaker, I realized it was Hazel.

"What are you doing in the men's bathroom?!? You're going to get caught!" I said, as I walked closer to her.

She grabbed me by my shoulders and pushed me into a nearby stall. I had no choice but to sit on the toilet, and I watched, as Hazel locked the door.

"Okay, this election is going to be bad. I mean, real bad. Mr. Rossi wants to win, and he is going to do it, with the help of his sons and close friends. I don't know what they are going to do, not exactly, but I am afraid that people are going to get hurt. I'm in this too…I have to be, but I'm telling you now because I know it is the right thing to do. All of those rumors about them working for the mafia, it's all true. Mr. Rossi is the leader of organized crime, and his kids are with him, all the way. I'm telling you, not Ulysses.

He's a loud mouth and acts without thinking. If they find out I told *anyone*...," Hazel stopped.

"Hazel, it's okay. You can trust me," I assured her. "Should we go to the police or something?" I asked.

"The police in this town are useless, and they won't investigate without solid proof. Plus, Mr. Rossi has some officers on his payroll, so I'm not even sure who we could trust. I decided to take the matter into my own hands. I want to stop them, with your help," Hazel said.

"Is there anything else you can tell me? Anything that could help us?"

"No...they don't tell me very much. I was just told that when it's time, I will be told where to go and what to do. And Pete, on Saturday, we all saw Rudolph at Leo's house, snooping along with Sean and Harper."

"They thought so...they tried to tell me, but I didn't listen...hey, do they have as many guns as Sean said?" I asked.

"They have more."

I looked at Hazel, not sure what to say. "So, we know they want to win," I said," and they'll do whatever it takes, which probably means hurting...maybe killing people...what then?"

"I don't know. But they have a plan to secure their win. They are going to skew the voting. On election day, they will have people at all the polls," Hazel explained. "I'm supposed to be at the largest polling location, but I'm not sure what they want me to do yet," Hazel continued. "I'm going to get as much evidence as possible, to prove that they are engaging in voter fraud. Hopefully, it will work and they will go to jail."

"What do you think will happen to you?" I ask. "Aren't you afraid of being charged with conspiracy?"

"I am hoping that by telling you and betraying them...well hopefully, that will be enough," Hazel responded.

"This is huge, Hazel. I'll keep an eye out during the election. We'll do what we can, to keep everyone safe," I said.

"Listen, we should leave. People might get suspicious, noticing that we have both been gone for awhile."

"Agreed. One at a time...I'll go first," Hazel said. She turned before leaving. "Hey, Pete...be careful." She turned around and faced me one more time, giving me a light kiss on the cheek.

And with that, she was gone. Hazel unlocked the stall

door and left the bathroom. I waited a moment before following. About thirty seconds later, I turned to my right and saw Sean walking down the hallway. Something about the look on his face told me that he was suspicious.

"Dude, the meeting is over. Where have you been? It's been almost twenty minutes since you left for the bathroom...what took you so long?" Sean demanded.

"I must have lost track of time...sorry," I said.

"That's bullshit! You never lose track of time; you've never been late or missed anything before," Sean said. "So, what have you really been up to for the last twenty minutes?

"Alright, if you really want to know, we need to go somewhere else to talk. There are too many people walking down these hallways for us to have this conversation," I said.

I walked into an empty dressing area behind stage, with Sean behind me, I closed and locked the door.

"It's this important that you have to lock us in a dressing room?" Sean asked.

"Yes, it's that important. Okay, where do I even start? I got finished using the bathroom and was about to wash my hands, when Hazel walked in and told me that we needed to talk..."

"Whoa, whoa, whoa, hold up a minute...Hazel stalked you in the men's bathroom?!? That is interesting!" Sean exclaimed.

"No wonder you didn't want anyone else to hear!"

"Don't be an ass, Sean! Let me finish! When I get done, you can think of all the dirty things you want, but there is some serious shit about to happen. I hate to say this, but you were right, okay? Hazel talked to me about the election...the Rossi's...they are in the mafia...she told me everything. They are rigging the election, but she wants us to stop them," I explained.

"Damn it! They *are* going to rig the election, which I already knew, thank you very much, and now Hazel has confirmed that they are definitely in the mafia. You didn't see those guns, Pete. This is really dangerous," Sean said.

"On election day, we have to go to the main polling place. Hazel doesn't know exactly what they are going to do, but the sheriff is going to be there," I said. "Hazel said we couldn't trust the police, but I think we can trust him."

"Sheriff Ray is going to be there? He's the only officer in town who actually cares about people," Sean said.

"If something goes down, and we try to stop it, I'm *sure* he'll help us. He has publicly voiced suspicions about the mafia but has never had enough proof," I responded. "If we tell him why we are there, it will give him the evidence he needs to prove that the mafia has been doing illegal stuff all along."

"I think it's better to go tell him now, so we can work with the police...we only have three days," Sean said.

"No, we're on our own." I opened the door, and we walked out into the hallway, joining the growing crowd of students, on their way to lunch.

7 VOTING CONSPIRACY

I walked down the hallway and went upstairs to my locker. I opened the door and saw my phone, just sitting there in front of everything else. Hazel must have pick pocketed me when I wasn't paying attention. I looked at my phone and nothing seemed to be changed on it; I never keep a password because I have nothing to hide. I grabbed my lunch as usual and walked down the stairs to the cafeteria, where the group was at. I saw where everyone else was sitting and sat right beside Ulysses.

"Okay, I have some more information about the election, and it's pretty serious. Some major stuff is going down, and it's up to us to stop it. Sheriff Ray is going to be at the election, and he may be able to help us. Hazel told me that Mr. Rossi is going to rig the election, to ensure a clean victory, and he is going to use his mafia connections to make it happen," I announced.

"Why were you with Hazel?" Ulysses asked?

Rudolph interrupted, "And more importantly, how can you even trust her? She's dating Leo, and you're trying to tell all of us that she is working *against* them!?!"

"Guys, I trust her, and I think you should too. She's the only chance we have at stopping the Rossi gang. The police in this town are useless, but I think that Sheriff Ray will work with us, no matter what. He always suspected they were working for the mafia but had no evidence to prove it," Sean said.

"I think I'm going to visit the police station, to see if we can get Sheriff Ray involved, without having to give too much away," I said. "I need to go right away; we can't afford to waste any time."

"That is a long walk from your house, dude," Harper said.

"Yeah, how are you planning to get there without a car?" Sean asked.

"As a matter of fact, I do have a car. I just don't use it very much, to save money on gas," I responded. "It's in the shed, right beside my house."

"This is huge! You've been hiding it in there, all this time?!?" Ulysses shouted.

"I kept it a secret so that I wouldn't have people constantly bugging me for rides...anyway, it can only hold three of us, so unfortunately, two of you have to stay behind. If just one of you wants to go, that works too," I said.

"Lucky for us, school is almost over, so once we leave, we can head to your place. We can see what your car looks like and then decide who is going," Harper teased.

Once the lunch period was over, we needed to head to our classes to finish off the day. We had our normal German studies, and once the bell rang, I headed out towards the front of the building, to wait for everyone else. After about six minutes of waiting, everyone else was heading out, and we started to walk to my place, everyone eager to see my car.

"It's about time the rest of you came out! I was waiting forever," I said.

"The hallway was crowded, as usual. You must get

out of German class early," Sean responded.

"Guys, enough talking! Get a move on it before it starts to get dark," Harper said.

We walked down the sidewalk from the high school through the suburban areas, passing a variety of homes and roads. We saw the Rossi brothers drive past us, with Hazel, and we watched them pull into their driveway. We walked a little bit more, and I was home with all of the others.

"Damn, your parents really are always gone, They never seem to be home," Ulysses stated.

"Like I said before, they go on vacation, they will be gone for the next week, so I'm all alone here," I said. "Anyways, lets go to the shed, so you can all have a look at my car."

"Yeah, I want to see this mysterious car of yours," Rudolph said.

"Whatever, you're just jealous. Just give me a minute...I have to go inside and grab the keys to the shed and car," I said.

I went inside and to the kitchen, where the keys were. I walked outside and saw the rest of the group standing in front of the shed.

"Ready to see something epic?" I asked, as I unlocked

the shed door.

"Let's see it," Harper said.

"Here we go...the best car I've ever owned," I said, as I pulled off the car cover to reveal the car to everyone.

"Is that even street legal? It looks like a bunch of random metal, all put together," Ulysses said.

"Is that from the 20s or something like that?" Sean asked.

"No, it's a general-purpose vehicle from the second world war. It still runs perfectly fine...I got it redone over the summer," I said. "It's a three-speed manual transmission."

"Well I'm not getting in that...no airbags, no seat belts," Ulysses said.

"Same...this thing looks like it has a zero percent survival rate," Sean echoed.

"You guys have no sense of fun. I'll go with you to the sheriff's office," Rudolph said, as he jumped in the passenger seat.

"I'll stay behind and help keep watch. We might even go on another spying mission while you are gone," Harper said.

"That would help us get more info, since the election is only three days away, but make sure you're careful, and *don't* let them see you this time. Let's go, Rudolph," I said.

I started the car and put it in first gear, hitting the gas. We went down the road and headed towards the Sheriff's office.

Because it was a three speed, I couldn't go very fast until we got onto the highway. Once we got there, I could push it to its maximum speed, 65 miles per hour.

"This isn't the best car to ride around in during the fall, even though global warming raised the temperature today to a balmy sixteen degrees Celsius," Rudolph commented.

"Tell me about it. I'm wearing shorts today because of this weather, and I never get to during November. I know that the Earth is slowly dying and we the people don't really care, but oh well, I'm not having children," I said.

"We've damaged Earth so much that scientists believe that we cannot stop the effects of climate change," Rudolph said.

"So, basically we can really only slow the effects of it now?" I asked.

"Yeah, pretty much. Earth is screwed," Rudolph said.

"You've got that right," I answered.

"Anyways, about Sheriff Ray, what is he like? I've never seen him before, not in person."

"He's a very nice person. He's one of those people who will follow the rules when needed and then push his luck other times, when he has to. He can't really be fired as the county sheriff, but he has gotten in trouble with the city mayor on multiple occasions," I explained.

"So, he's not a total asshole...that's good. What theories does he have about a mafia in Dutchville?" Rudolph asked.

"He has always suspected it but has never had any evidence, not until now. With this, I know he'll be willing to help us out, to catch them. Even if we never told him, he probably still would have been on the lookout for them, during the voting," I said. "But with our help, maybe he can actually put a stop to them."

After about an hour of driving down the highway, we turned off the exit and made our way through the small town of Adamstown. We located the sheriff's building and pulled right into the open space. We got out of the car and made our way into the sheriff's office, where Sheriff Ray was seated at his desk, doing some paperwork. Even seated, you could tell he was short, probably 5'8, but compelling. His short ginger hair protruded into small points at the top of his faded crew cut.

"What brings you two young gentlemen into my office this afternoon?" Sheriff Ray asked, looking directly at us with his ocean blue eyes.

"Good afternoon, Sheriff Ray. I'm Pete Mailer, and this is Rudolph Kowalski. We are from Dutchville, and we came here to bring you some important information about the upcoming elections," I said.

"Go ahead, I'm all ears," Ray said.

"I have gotten word that the Mafia is going to rig the election so their leader, Mr. Rossi will become the new school board president. I got this information from someone who is close to the Rossi gang, but who is secretly working against them. She didn't want me to come to you before election day, but I think we can count on you, sir," I explained.

"The Mafia?!? I knew it! All along the Mayor thought I was some crazy old sheriff who didn't know better than him, but I'll show him now, that no good piece of shit mayor!" Ray exploded. "Forgive my language you two, but I *hate* it when people doubt me, especially when I know, *for a fact,* that I am correct! When this thing breaks, he'll be exposed for the ignorant fool he really is."

"We need you to help us catch them, in the act. Our informant is going to tip us off to their specific whereabouts and activities," I said.

"Alright, boys, I've got your backs. Let me know where I need to be, in order to expose how they've meddled in this election, and I'll go in for the arrest. I will make sure I get their father too. I'm *not* going to let him get away," Ray proclaimed to all of us.

"I'm so glad you can help us out. We knew there was a mafia, like you, but we've never had any solid proof until now. This time, we have them right where we want them!" Rudolph exclaimed.

Sheriff Ray stood up and walked to the door, "You kids get a move on; it's starting to get dark outside. You can count on me to bring them to justice. I'll make sure that I follow up with you at home too. Thanks for trusting me...I always knew there was mafia in this county. Some folks thought it was just my imagination running away with me," Ray told us, as he opened the door letting us out.

"Have a nice night, Sheriff. Hope to see you on

election day," I breathed.

"You too. Drive safely, especially in that old car. Well actually, that car looks like a tank! You'll be fine...just drive the speed limit and stay safe," Ray called.

The ride back home was almost silent. By the time we got back, it was about seven o'clock and already dark outside. Once we got to my house, I turned off my car and went inside to see the rest of the gang, sitting in the kitchen, waiting for us to arrive.

"How was the journey to Adamstown? You were gone long enough," Ulysses noted.

"It was really good. Sheriff Ray was in his office, and he is fully on board with our plan to expose the mafia. He will definitely be here on election day," I responded.

"When you two were gone, I was thinking about this, and there is something I can't figure out. There has to be a reason why they're going to do this. The mayor has to be involved," Sean said.

"What if the mayor and Ottavio are both working together to win? If Ottavio wins, maybe McCreedy will benefit," Ulysses said. "If Ottavio gains popularity in the town, as board president, he might become the next mayor. That would give McCreedy the chance to become a Representative for the 8th district for the Commonwealth. If he makes connections with the mafia, by helping Ottavio get elected to the school board, he will have more money and more power. Then lower state New York will invade our town, bringing crime with it."

"We can't let that happen to our town! We need to stop them, and that is why Sheriff Ray is going to help us beat them," I said.

"The Sheriff is basically the only person who can save the town. The local police is probably working with the mayor and won't listen to us," Rudolph said.

"It's getting late...let's all head out for the night. Tomorrow will be a normal school day, but during study hall, we need to meet up and start coming up with some solid strategies," Sean said.

"In that case, I will see all of you guys tomorrow. Have a safe trip back home," I said, as I walked towards the door, opening it for all of them.

8 SHERIFF'S PLAN

I saw my phone in the middle of the night light up with a message, from someone I didn't know. It was Hazel. The message read, *Did you tell the sheriff about our plan?* I responded by saying, *Yes, he is on board with this...he will there on election day to bust them.* I couldn't stay up long enough to see the next message, but I knew her reply would be waiting for me the next morning.

The next day I woke up and started to get ready for school as usual, ignoring my phone for awhile in the process. Once I got done with everything, I looked at my phone and was surprised to see no new messages from Hazel, or from anyone. I grabbed my car keys and walked out the door. Starting towards my car, I saw Ulysses and Sean walking down the sidewalk towards me.

"Looks like you're driving to school today. We might as well hitch a ride along with you," Sean said.

"Oh, I thought you too were too afraid to ride with me, since you think it's just a boneless car frame. Fine, whatever. Just jump in, but there are no seat belts," I said.

"Danger, danger everywhere...this car isn't safe anyway. I'm still surprised it's even street legal. Make sure you don't drive too fast. I want to live past seventeen," Ulysses said.

"There nothing to worry about. It doesn't go very fast. You just need to be careful on the road. There can be a lot of assholes out there, especially the out of state drivers you see up here," I respond, as I started the car.

I pulled out on into the street and we made our way to school.

"Tomorrow is the election. I hope all of us are ready for the shit that is going to go down with the police," Sean said.

"What if the Rossi brothers have guns on them? What if this turns into a shoot-out?" Ulysses asked.

"Yeah, that's totally possible. After all, they are the mafia," Sean responded.

We pulled up to an intersection where the red light takes forever, and the next car that pulled up right beside us was the good old mustang belonging to Leo Rossi, driving with his brother in the passenger's side.

"Hey, look who's beside us. I have a great idea, and you guys will love it!" I said, starting to rev my engine up.

"What are you doing? If you think you're racing, they are totally going to beat us," Ulysses said.

"No, they're not. You'll see what he's doing...look behind us." Sean looked towards the back and pointed to Sheriff Ray's cruiser.

"Oh, I see..." Ulysses noted.

As the light turned green, their car zoomed off into the distance, followed by Sheriff Ray's car, turning on his lights. I continued at the regular speed, passing their car as it was stopped by the Sheriff. We all laughed and pulled into the school parking lot. We all went our separate ways for the first twenty minutes, before school officially started. I wandered through the hallways, looking at the walls to look for updated posters and campaign information. I turned around and saw Sheriff Ray walk into the office. He waved at me, and I waved back, continuing my journey down the hallway. The hallway was unusually crowded, considering it was before the first bell. People around me were staring, but I acted like I didn't notice.

"Hey Pete, forget to shave your face again?" someone asked as I walked down the hallway and up the stairs.

"I always forget to do that! Watch, I'll forget tomorrow also."

"Hey, you made it to school early! You must have driven," Harper said.

"Yeah, it was actually decent outside, and I thought it would be nice drive to school. Sean and Ulysses tagged along for the ride. Where is Rudolph? I'm guessing he's here somewhere, but I didn't see him leave his house this morning. I did leave a little late though," I said to him.

"We'll talk later. I have to get to my locker and my classes. See you at lunch I guess," Harper said, walking down the stairs.

I continued my way up the stairs, passing people, and walked down the hall to get to my locker. I opened it and started to put things in. I walked into physics class about ten minutes early, and Mr. Cannon wasn't in the room. In the meantime, I just sat there and looked my phone to check if anything new was going on. I didn't see anything that amounted to much. The stock market closed the previous day, with closings lower than expected. The date was Tuesday November 17, and the stock market was opening at 9 A.M. Investors were looking at a higher open, they hoped. More people were slowly walking into physics class, and at the end of the line I saw Rudolph walk in, and he sat right beside me, as usual.

"Where were you at? Harper was looking for you earlier," I asked.

"I was walking into the building after you guys got in, and Sheriff Ray wanted to talk with me in the conference room. He wants all of the people involved in this to meet him during study hall before lunch," Rudolph answered. "He said that he is making a plan for tomorrow's election and how we can help him. If anyone asks, we are to say that he is talking to us about school security, since we are on the student board."

"Alright, this is good. We need a plan of action, so that there isn't a scene," I responded.

The clock arms hit eight o'clock, and Mr. Cannon started to walk in, so that he could take attendance. You could hear all of the footsteps in the hallway, echoing into the room. Mr. Cannon walked over to the door, shuts it, and stood in front of the class with a marker in hand.

"Today is Tuesday, and since this election is so important, We are encouraging anyone at or above the age of 18 to vote," Mr. Cannon announced to everyone. "I hope to see all of the student board members there, to witness the election process. Staff will also be there, to monitor voting and to clean up after the voters."

Mr. Cannon sat back down at his desk and gave us the remainder of the class to complete assignments. Some people talked and others stayed quiet. Most of the kids were talking about the election.

"Since we don't have a lot of work, we might as well think of some suggestions for Sheriff Ray," Rudolph said.

"I don't know...he's the sheriff and knows what is best. We should probably follow his lead. Anyways, I've been thinking about it, and there is a chance that this election could be postponed, if Sheriff Ray thinks that it isn't going to be safe," I said. "Just make sure you don't start anything with the Rossi's. Act like everything's normal."

After class ended, we all left the room. I walked down the hallway and moved through the crowd of people to get to College Algebra. Sean was already sitting down, Wilson wasn't in the room yet.

"Hey, Rudolph told me that Sheriff Ray wanted to see all of us during the first study hall and that before lunch, he is going to talk to us about his plans for election day," I announced.

"That's good. We can finally bust those grease monkeys and put an end to gang activity. On a side note, Pete, you have been acting really strange the last couple of days. You still never told me what happened to you and Ulysses on Friday night when we were gone...so what happened?" Sean asked.

"Fine, I'll tell you...we have some time. When you guys left, we sat on the couch talking about things...and then I told him that I went to the doctor's...and I let him read the report with my diagnosis. After I told him, he just stared and me...but then he just smiled at me," I answered.

"So...what's wrong with you?" Sean asked.

"Can you just drop it for now? The bell is about to ring anyway."

"Sure, whatever."

In class there was a quiz, covering material from the previous week. Wilson wasn't at school, so it was just Sean and I. The test wasn't hard at all – I just had to think and explain what I was doing. I turned in my test to Ms. Ray and sat back down in my chair, waiting patiently for the period to end.

Once the bell rang I left the room in a hurry, to get across to the other side of the building and reach the health room before I was late. As I was walking down the hallway on the first floor, I met up with Ulysses.

"Whenever I get the chance, we need to talk later today, after school, most likely at my house, if you can make it," I stammered.

"Okay, I can make it over," Ulysses said.

We hurried into the classroom to take our seats. "Welcome everyone. Sorry I wasn't in yesterday – I was a little sick, but I feel better now," Mrs. Lungo announced to all of us. "Today, we are going to do more research on the way drugs affect the human mind. For this, we are going to get into pairs and do research on different types of drugs."

To me, the subject was frustrating. If a person had even a sliver of common sense, they would know that drugs are not good for your health...but I know that peer pressure can get to people. Ulysses and I are lucky because we never get pressured to do anything. We have decent friends who care mostly about our well-being.

Mrs. Lungo got a phone call on the school phone and she picked it up. We all got quiet so she could hear what they were saying, and from what I could see, it must have been from the office due to the extension showing on the caller ID.

"Pete and Ulysses, you are needed in the office," Mrs. Lungo said.

I got up from my seat and walked out the door. Ulysses followed behind and closed the door. As we walked down the hall to the office, we met up with Sean, Rudolph, and Harper. Sheriff Ray opened the door for us, and we all walked in.

"I'm glad all of you made it. Follow me to the conference room, where we will have some privacy," Sheriff Ray said.

We took our seats across from Sheriff Ray, and he grabbed a stack of papers he had been working on for the last couple of hours.

"Alright Sheriff, what's the plan?" Rudolph asked.

"For this, we need even numbers, so having six of us

here is perfect. You are going to be stationed at the various polling locations, and your job will be to alert me, as soon as you see anything suspicious," Ray said.

"So, what do we do then?" I asked.

"If you see anything, you radio me immediately," Ray answered. "Then you get out of there. Leave the rest to me. I don't want you boys putting yourselves in any danger."

"But Rudolph and I could totally take them down! We have the height and strength to stop them, even Mr. Rossi," Harper said.

"No, absolutely not. If you want to help, this is nonnegotiable. And as far as Mr. Rossi is concerned, we need to make sure that his whereabouts are known the entire day. I'm hoping we can count on Hazel for that. Once I have enough evidence, I'll move in to make the arrest," Ray said.

"Sounds like a good plan, Sheriff," Ulysses said. "This will be good."

"I wish we could do more, but regardless, we are doing something good for the town and school," I said.

"Stay safe boys," Sheriff said.

The idea sounded great, but the actual details of the day were concerning to me. Ultimately, I wasn't too worried. We had the law on our side to save us.

"Go back to your classes and enjoy the rest of your day," Ray said.

We left the conference room and the office, and by the looks of the halls, it was now study hall.

"Don't worry guys. They won't get away with this...trust me," Harper said, and he walked away with Rudolph and Ulysses.

9 CONSIGLIERE INTERROGATION

The rest of the day seemed normal to me. We talked about life and other things at lunch, not discussing the plan because too many people were around us. Once school got out, I went to the front of the building with Rudolph and Sean...Ulysses and Harper still didn't want to ride in my car. We made our way back to my place, and then we parted ways in preparation for the election. I walked inside of my house, where it was quiet and calm. I went upstairs to check my emails and other news around town and statewide. By the looks of it, the election was dominating all other news, as it should have.

I walked back down the stairs to sit on the couch and

watch the news, to get more updates. It was the same old stuff: car accidents, death, fire, etc. But I still sat there and watched it, it was always interesting to me.

After about fifteen minutes of watching the news, I turned off the TV and went back upstairs to lay down. Recent events at school had taken a toll on me, and I couldn't stay up very long. I went back into my room and laid on my bed and closed my eyes.

I woke up to the sound of the doorbell ringing. I got up from my bed and made my way back down the steps, to open the front door. It was Hazel.

"What are you doing here?" I asked.

"Like you don't know. We need to talk," she responded.

Hazel walked in without me saying anything and sat down on the couch. At least I could comfort myself with the knowledge that she wasn't a vampire, or she would've never done that. I closed the door behind her and made my way to the living room.

"Do you want anything? Like water, juice? No milk because I'm lactose intolerant, but there is almond milk," I offered.

"No, I'm good. I just want to talk," she said.

Sitting down in front of her I started, "What do you

want to talk about specifically? What's wrong?" I asked. "Is there something going on we need to know about, any news about the Rossi's plans for tomorrow?"

"Just shut up and listen to me. I'm pissed at you! You're sneaky, manipulative, and a liar. You promised me you wouldn't go to the police and then all of a sudden, Sheriff Ray shows up at school?!?"

"But..."

"No, don't try to bullshit me. Your friends already told me some lame-ass story about how he wanted to discuss school security with you. You have a real mental problem, you know that?"

"Hazel...I'm...I just thought it was best...I just want to keep everyone safe..."

"You still don't get it, do you? I am involved with the *Rossi* family. I trusted you. I looked into you, and you know what I found out?" letting her question linger. "You're a psychopath."

"You had no right to do that! That's my personal business! It's not even that bad...it's just a stupid label!"

"Yeah, well you just proved that it's true. You care about no one but yourself. You might be able to manipulate your stupid little friends, but not me,"

Hazel said.

"Okay, look I wanted to make sure everyone was going to be safe, what you told me about…everything we've seen…if Ray never knew about this, they would win, and what would happen to this town?"

"No, I told you not to tell the police! Can't you not understand that?! You're just like Ulysses, not being able to keep secrets!" she yelled.

"Then why tell me?!" I yelled back.

Hazel thought for a moment. "I got cold feet about the plan they had. I just felt like it was wrong. What they do now, I can live with that. If they become more powerful…I don't know…when I told you, I felt better talking to someone. After that I realized that I shouldn't have told anyone, that I was betraying Leo, and the rest of the family. So I asked you to keep it from the police, I never want Leo to find out, and if he ever got taken away…" she paused, looking at me.

"Look, I can hide things for a long time, but when you told me that, I knew I had to tell someone about it. They are committing *fraud*, Hazel…and I don't think they are afraid to hurt people to win. And if… I don't know. The rise of evil only happens if the good people don't act on it. If I didn't say something, this town would become trashed. They would bring in evil and shady business men...crime would increase and there would be murders," I said.

"I know you tried to do good, but no, just no," she said.

"What's wrong?" I asked.

"Nothing...I'm just pissed about what you did yesterday and today," she said.

"There is obviously something else, I can forgive you about being mad at me for telling the police, but I had to...it was the right thing for me to do. My parents always told me to do that. Now, tell me what is wrong," I said.

"Okay, the real reason I have become so close to the Rossi family is because my parents suck. They don't give a shit about me. They are never around, and when they do bother to show up, they aren't happy with anything that I do. I hate them... so I spend most of my time at the Rossi house. They actually care about me..." "Well, did you ever talk to a counselor at school or something like that? You can get help with that, family counseling?" I asked.

"No, they would never listen to me. I'm eighteen now, and I can do whatever I want. I don't need them. I have a long life ahead of me, college for example," she said.

I rubbed my hands together to make some kind of sound, to dissolve the moment of silence. I also fixed my hair, brushing it to the left, staying involved in the conversation.

"So, what about college?" I asked.

"Leo and I are getting serious, and Mr. Rossi wants me to get more involved in their lives. He's been talking to me about college for me and his kids. I want to go into law and psychology, he wants to support me, so that I can help with their business whenever I get out of college. He says I'm already family."

"Interesting…I might add, you have your entire life ahead of you."

"I know, I do have second thoughts sometimes, but I *really* like Leo…and the rest of the family is great too," Hazel said.

"You have to do what you feel is right. It's not my life, it's yours, and life is a special thing. Make the memories you will always remember, in life and death," I said.

"That's really nice of you to say," Hazel said.

"You can be anyone you want to be, but the best person to be is just yourself. Be better than what people tell you, your parents, Mr. Rossi, and even Leo. You will do perfectly fine on the road ahead of you."

"Thanks, I really appreciate it. I can't mad at my big ginger guy friend for very long," she smiled. "You were always special to me..."

"How so?" I asked.

"You're different from the rest of your friends."

I sat back in my chair and waited for her to continue.

"Ulysses is the type of person who problem solves to help everyone. He's the strange one out of your friends, though. He keeps secrets you know. Then there's Sean. Sean is so negative, and he's a racist. No one likes him, other than your group of friends, and a few others that know him. No wonder he has graying hair at seventeen – being pissed off at the world will do that to you. Harper, the Scottish one, he's a very powerful person, and people are afraid of him. Leo and Stefano do not like him at all. He looks like a person who could win any fight, and his accent is scary when you get him angry. I've seen him help people though, when they need it, and he doesn't do it for personal gain. Lastly is Rudolph, the adrenaline junkie who will do anything risky for fun. He isn't afraid of much, and because he's six feet tall, he's a danger to Leo and Stefano."

"Wait, what do you mean, Ulysses is a strange person? Isn't everyone strange in their own way?" I asked.

"Yes, but he's different..."

"How so?"

"He...acts feminine sometimes. Haven't you ever picked up on that? I think he's gay..."

"No, not really. Even if he does, so what? Acting feminine doesn't automatically make him gay. He's dated girls in the past! He even really liked some of them, he told me. He says that girls are hot all the time!" I counterclaim.

"Okay fine, maybe he isn't gay after all, but he's not straight," she said to me.

"So, what? He's bisexual or something?" I asked.

"You're not very observant, are you?"

"Maybe I should've noticed more...he's always acted strange around me...but he played it off, as if he was just normally weird. Do you think he likes me?" I ask.

"Bingo, correct! Now you just have to read the signals coming your way and react," she said.

"That sucks. I literally have no clue when it comes to

this stuff, as you already know."

"Listen, it's really not that hard. You can just say you're interested or not, and move on…it won't be that bad," she said. "If you're worried about being Catholic, don't be. It doesn't really matter what anybody else thinks…and you're a good person, which is what really counts."

"I don't know…I need time to think about all of this."

"Why?"

"I'm down with that, it's just another person. Who's going to really judge? It's the twenty first century…change is good, and there is no way to stop it," I said. "Plus, every relationship I have had with a girl has gone south. What am I supposed to do, hook up with another one and deal with same problems?"

"You and Ulysses would make a good couple, you know. You have things in common, like politics," she said. "Some people already think that."

"I'm glad you talked to me about this – thanks for being a good friend."

"I won't judge, people at school don't judge, nearly everyone is accepting," she said to me. "You can tell him if you want…it would make him happier than what he is…or you can keep it a secret until he decides to tell you."

"I'll think about it, but you're the only person who really knows about this," I told her.

"Okay good," she said.

At this point, my face was already bright red, and I couldn't hide it. I just had to sit and relax.

"So…how was your day at school?" Hazel asked.

"It was fine…let's talk about something else," I answered. "So, if I ever worked for the mafia, what rank would I hold in the tree of power? And how does that all work? You know all about it from being so close with the Rossis."

"Okay, let me put it in terms of your friends. The leader of organized crime would be…Ulysses, or you, depending on who is better at logic and practices. If Ulysses was Kingpin, you would definitely be the Underboss. The Godfather is considered the ultimate leader of the organization and will always have the most influence. They will make the decisions for the family. Underboss is the second in command in the family. They will carry out all of the Godfather's wishes and will observe day to day operations, kinda like a supervisor in stores. The other members do the dirty work that is needed, and if the Godfather is arrested, killed, or is absent for some reason, unable to hold power, the Underboss is promoted to the leader, unless the Godfather instructed that there would be another Godfather in place of him. Since Sean is basically a walking target, he would be the adviser or consigliere. He does give good advice, when moments are tough, and it is actually good. Consigliere is an adviser for the Godfather, not a family member but a close and trusted person the Godfather knows. Most consiglieres are lawyers. Harper and Rudolph, since they are not originally from here, they would be considered members of the Caporegime, carrying out the orders of the Godfather and Underbosses but mostly the underbosses. Because the Godfather is in charge of the business, he would just send orders down to the Underboss, then to the Capos. That keeps the heat off of him. The Underboss goes out and does the dirty work. He says and sends orders and deals with other stuff," Hazel went on and on.

"So, if my group of friends had our own family, with Ulysses in charge, if something happened to him, I would be Godfather?" I asked.

"Yes and no. It's complicated and depends on the exact circumstances. Every soldier you would have recruited would need believe that you're the Godfather and not Ulysses, in case there was a rat, selling out Ulysses and the organization. The real Godfather can recover quickly, as long as trusted members haven't been caught."

"Oh, I see now. So, you're saying that Leo's father is the true Kingpin of the business, and if he gets caught, Leo would become the mafia leader, and all of the other roles would be shifted to counteract the missing role?" I asked.

"Yes, you've got it. If Ottavio would get arrested, Leo would get promoted to the Godfather and would take control immediately, which is good and also bad for them. If promoted, he would be able to look out for the best interests of the family, which is good. The bad part would be his age and inexperience. He would be brand new and would have to deal with the older officials and his consigliere. He would have a lot of enemies too. I don't know what will happen next, but I worry about Leo. It might actually be Ottavio's Underboss who will become the Godfather," Hazel said. "I don't know... it's a lot to think about, and now that the sheriff is involved..."

"Hazel, I really do appreciate that you can

understand what is going on here. All five of us kinda knew that you people worked for the mafia, but you told me that it is true. I hope you believe me when I say that I don't want anyone to get hurt."

Hazel looked away for a moment before speaking. "Anything else you want to talk about, that doesn't relate to the mafia or crime?" Hazel asked me.

"It's getting late…I think you should go before it gets any later than it is now or Leo finds out that you are gone," I said.

"No, I don't think I will. I'm going to stay here for the night…I know your parents are not here. You made a big scene that they're on vacation, which means that I can stay and hang out, keep you some company," she said.

"Well crap, I can't say no to that. Where do you want to sleep at?" I asked her, while standing back up.

"What about in your room?" she asked.

"Okay, I'll take the other guest bedroom then," I said.

"No…you're going to sleep with me, in your room," she said.

"Uh no, that's weird. You know, Leo would kill me," I objected.

"You'll be fine. We can keep talking, in your room,"

she explained.

"Alright, if you say so," I said.

I walked up the stairs and guided her to my room, and we entered the room. She closed the door right behind her. I went over to my desk and sat on the chair, and she sat on my bed. I started to take off my shoes.

"So, now we're up here in my room," I said to her.

"You know, you are kinda hot...your hair is perfectly orange," she said. "Tall and broad shoulders, good enough to defend people, to protect the ones you care about."

"Yeah, I get that a lot in school. Girls do like that," I told her.

"If I wasn't with Leo, I'd probably date you. Since you're not with Erin, there could be a possibility," she said.

"What do you mean?" I asked.

"Leo *can* be annoying...he's strict, and I don't get to have any fun with my other friends. I'm getting kind of tired of it," she explained.

"Talk to him; he'd probably understand," I said.

"No, he thinks he knows everything, which I hate so much," she said.

"Oh, I see. Then, why don't you leave him?" I asked.

"If I leave him, I think he will snap and go on a rampage, along with his brother," she explained. "He has the worst temper on Earth."

"You can't fix that," I said.

"That's why I'm here, you know. You listen to me, and you don't get angry as fast...which totally gives me the upper hand," she said.

"Well...thanks..."

"We should talk more. We could end up having a lot in common that we don't know about," she said.

"We probably do," I told her.

Hazel stood up and grabbed my hand, pulling me down with her. I sat on my bed, with her sitting playfully on my lap.

"Okay, what are you trying to do?" I asked.

"You know what? Instead of talking about boring stuff, we should continue our conversation about your messed-up relationship ideology. If you and Ulysses ever dated, what would you guys do?" Hazel asked.

"I don't know, but I do have standards," I said.

"Like what?" she asked. "I mean, I know how you feel about Ulysses, but what about girls?"

"Alright, in a girl, I would give them basically all of

the power. I like strong women, women who aren't afraid to defend themselves."

"Okay," Hazel said, wrapping her arms around me, "what about guys?"

"In guys, it's kinda weird. I like to be the one with the power."

"And…what about hair?" she asked.

"Style doesn't really matter; I like color. My favorite colors are ginger and brown, of any shade. Not particularly fond of blonde or dyed hair," I said.

"I see…what else do you like? Like sex for a start?" she asked.

"I don't know," I told Hazel. "I don't know if I'm ready to have sex with a man…but I definitely would with a woman."

"I'm glad to hear that," she smiled. "But what if Ulysses wants it?" she asked.

"He's not getting it, sorry…we can do anything else but that," I said.

"If I were single…would you try and hook up with me?"

"Probably…you seem like you can stand your ground, you're easy to talk with, and you know a lot, which I like. You are hot, not going to lie about that," I smiled back.

"That's nice of you to say...I like getting complements."

"I give women all of my respect...they deserve all of it," I said.

"Good...you know, you would make a great lover, giving women respect and the way you listen..."

Hazel got off my lap and slowly walked around the bed, towards the door. I stood up and followed behind her.

"What are you doing?" I asked. "I thought you were staying..."

"I am...you're sleeping me with," she said.

"Whoa, no! I'm not sleeping with you...I can't do that!"

"Calm down, will you? I'm not like that. I just want to sleep with you...I don't like being alone," she paused, taking my hand. "Just come downstairs with me, so I can get my things."

We both changed and got into bed. We were both asleep in seconds.

10 ELECTION DAY

"Last night was a very strange night for me," I said.

"Why? Did something happen last night that I missed?" Sean asked.

"Yeah, you missed quite a lot. She told me a lot, and she gave her opinions about all of us too. Of course, she made a big deal about you being rude all of the time," I half joked.

"Oh well, as long as I'm happy, that's all that matters," Sean said. "Where is everyone else? School was out ten minutes ago."

"They'll be out sooner than later. Ulysses is probably talking to Mr. Mickelson about the election, and Rudolph is probably wondering the hallways. I don't know about Harper; he can be gone for a while then be right back in seconds," I said.

"We should just wait a little bit longer for them, since the building doesn't fully close until five," Sean said.

"Did you hear everyone was talking about the election today? They seem excited about changing the face of the school," I said.

"They're in for a rude awakening. The state is going to be pissed when this is investigated. This will definitely make headlines," Sean said.

"Sheriff Ray should already be at the city hall for his election. Once everyone gets out here, we can make our way there," I said.

As we discussed the election and the news, Rudolph walked out of the building with a couple of band-aids on his fingers.

"What did you do this time?" I asked.

"I was at the nurse's office for a while. I got superglue stuck on my fingers, and I couldn't get it off of me...Wilson dared me to do it, so I did. It was for twenty dollars and was totally worth it," Rudolph explained.

"What a fucking idiot!" Sean yelled. "At least you didn't eat it or put it in your hair."

"Well, twenty dollars is twenty dollars, you know," I said.

"Wilson offered double if I put in my hair, but I was smart enough to say no to that," Rudolph said.

"Yeah, that was smart," I said.

"This is getting annoying. Ulysses and Harper are taking *forever* to get down here. Did you see them as you were walking out of the building?" Sean asked Rudolph, who wasn't even paying attention to him.

"Oh, what? Yeah, I did see them when I was walking. Ulysses said that he was going to talk to Mr. Mickelson and told me to tell you that he will see you at the polls later today. Harper is also with him. We can leave now, before it gets colder outside," Rudolph said.

Sean sighed in anger as he faced me and started to walk towards the sidewalk, in the direction of home.

"You know you could have told us that when you were walking out, instead of standing here talking about your stupid bet," Sean angrily said to Rudolph.

"I thought the bet was more interesting, and I thought that they told you about their plans before school was out. But now we all know, and we can go," Rudolph said, as he got closer to Sean.

We walked away from the school and onto the sidewalk. The roads were very quiet, almost too quiet. There were absolutely no cars on the roads. It was a Wednesday, still the work week.

"This seems spooky, no cars on the road. It's getting foggy too… something out of a horror movie," I said.

"I'm guessing that most people are getting ready for the election and decided to stay off the road for the day. And the town isn't very big, only about 30,000 people. That doesn't make it a big city," Rudolph said.

"Maybe there was a mass frenzy at some store or even a traffic backup on the highway," Sean said.

"I doubt there was some accident on the highway, but I think it's because it's almost 4 o'clock, and the election is at 5:30," I said.

"Big town, small city, it doesn't matter. There is nobody out today, other than a few cars here and there," Sean said.

"You know this whole election fraud thing is a joke. Why would they even rig an election that he's going to win anyway?" Rudolph asked.

"They're greedy, and they want a landslide election, so he is guaranteed to win without any suspicion. Plus, if he lost, a lot of people would be upset," Sean explained to Rudolph.

"Why don't we just let him win then?" Rudolph asked.

Sean stopped in his tracks, "You idiot! What they are doing is totally illegal! And did you forget, they are a part of the Mafia?!?"

"Oh, I forgot about that," he said.

"You know, after all of these years of knowing you, I'm not surprised anymore, truly not. I've just gotten used to your dumbness," I said.

"We are almost home. Once we get to your place, we have to wait until we hear from Harper or Ulysses. They will tell us which polling place to go to, along with Sheriff Ray," Sean said. "That's when our plan will start."

We finally got to my house and settled in. I went to the kitchen to get water. Sean and Rudolph made their way to the living room to sit down. I made my way to the living room and sat on the chair facing the kitchen, and Sean and Rudolph sat on the couch facing me.

"We just wait for the word," Sean said.

"I guess so," I said.

"We should do something fun in the meantime," Rudolph said.

"What should we do? Any ideas?" Sean asked.

"Don't look at me. I have no clue," I said.

"How about we fight in the meantime?" Rudolph suggested.

"Fight? No, I don't want to fight," Sean said.

"Oh, come on. It will be fun. Plus, it's good defense practice," I said.

"Come on, you might actually enjoy yourself," Rudolph said.

"Okay fine, what could go wrong? Just take it easy...I don't want to get more hurt than the last time we did this," Sean said.

We all agreed to go outside to the backyard, where we could have a fighting match. We stood in a circle to get ready.

"So, who is first to go?" I asked.

"How about me and you fight first, and then Sean can take the winner," Rudolph said. "It's only fair because he didn't want to do it in the first place."

Rudolph and I backed up about five feet and got ready. Sean gave the okay, and we charged at each other. Rudolph was knocked off his feet immediately, and I followed suit.

"Shit, you're too good at this stuff," Rudolph said.

"Rudolph, you should go clean yourself off. I can see blood running down from your ears," Sean said.

We went back inside after an anticlimactic fight to clean up after ourselves. We had to be presentable.

"You know, after talking with Sheriff Ray, I wonder why the Mayor of our town forced him to stop investigating the suspected mafia. He was close to getting them years ago," I said.

"The Mayor is corrupt just like them! He's probably working with the mafia to make sure he stays in power. Also, politicians are all corrupt, no matter what they say. Trust me, I know," Sean said.

"I think we should head out," Rudolph said.

"I'm with you. We can take my car, and Sean, you have to ride in it…it's not going to kill you," I said.

Sean sighed, "Alright, fine. I can deal with it for one day, I guess."

We left my house and got into my car, driving right into downtown Dutchville where people were gathered around the city hall building, including the town police and Sheriff Ray. Ulysses and Harper were there waiting for us. We parked our car about two blocks away from city hall and started to walk. It was actually starting to get cold out, and I regretted wearing shorts.

"Hey, we just passed an alley where I saw two people talking. They could be some mafia associates," Rudolph teased.

"Just keep walking. Go faster before they realize that you looked at them and suspect that we know what is going on," Sean said.

"Don't worry about it. We are in eyesight of Sheriff Ray," I said.

"Maybe it was some drug dealers. Who cares? It was just some people in an alleyway, we have better things to do," Rudolph said.

"You brought it up in the first place," I said.

We met up with Ulysses and Harper inside of the election rooms, with Sheriff Ray behind them.

"Alright, good. You all made it to the election on time, and people are starting to fill into the booths for voting," Ray announced. "Once most of the voting is finished, our plan will begin."

"Look, there he is...that Mafia leader guy," Rudolph said.

"Shut up! We cannot afford to blow the plan right now, you dumbass mammal!" Sean yelled.

"I was just making an observation, chill," Rudolph

responded.

"Just keep your thoughts to yourself. Don't say anything unless it's actually important," I said.

We took a seat away from the voting booths and waited for people to vote and move on with their day. We had to find out where the voting ballots were being stored because none of us knew where they were taking them, including Sheriff Ray.

Around seven o'clock, we saw the very first batch of votes being transported to the press room, where conferences were held and results were discussed with the local news.

"There it is, the room for the votes to be counted. We need to find the Sheriff," Ulysses said. "The ringleaders have to be in there."

I stood up and told Harper to follow me to find Sheriff Ray. We looked around the building and found him talking to Jake, the school janitor.

"It was nice talking to you Jake. I'll see you later." Sheriff Ray turned to us, "Did you boys find out where they are storing the votes?" Ray asked.

"Yes, we did. It's the conference room," I said. "They are there, right now."

"Good work. You boys go home. We've got it from

here." Sheriff Ray stopped Jake, "Hey Jake, do you have the keys to the conference room?"

Jake set his mop against the wall and walked towards the conference room, as Sheriff Ray gathered other officers, who were standing around waiting for his orders.

"Everyone, listen up. We have suspected voter fraud and mafia activity being coordinated from the conference room, where the votes are being counted. We have to go in and stop them before the votes are finalized," Ray announced. "It's time."

Sheriff Ray ordered a squad to run to the other side of the building, passing through people as well as the other officers, in search of Ottavio. Harper and I saw them, and followed, at a distance. I stopped to see everyone else near the door, waiting for Jake to open it. We saw the Mayor walk over to us immediately, looking distressed at the unfolding events.

"What on Earth are you people doing in front of the conference room? That room is supposed to be locked until the votes are finalized! You cannot walk in there! Under no circumstances are you to enter that room!" he yelled at all of us.

"I'm going in whether you like it or not," Ray yelled,

as he kicked in the door himself, before Jake could open the door for him. Ray stormed into the room with his gun in hand, at the ready.

"Police motherfuckers! You're all under arrest! Put your hands up, right now!" Sheriff Ray yelled.

"What are you doing?!?" the Mayor exclaimed. He stopped and stared, as the Rossi family was exposed to everyone.

"Ottavio Rossi," Sheriff Ray started, "you are under arrest for fraud and conspiracy. You have…"

Leo shouted, cutting the Sheriff off. He reached behind his back, to unholster his gun but was tackled to the ground by Ray's backup. He looked at the crowed and locked eyes with me. He looked murderous.

Everyone in the building was shocked, and in a matter of minutes, six prominent members of the community were arrested, including the Mayor of the city himself. Jake walked over to Sheriff Ray, with a knowing look.

"Before anything happens, Weston, I want you to know that I work for the FBI, and I have been investigating this suspected mafia for about two years. Someone finally made a solid connection and pushed for an arrest, and I want to thank you."

"Well, I'll be damned," Sheriff Ray said, as he shook hands with Jake. "Sure glad you were here."

"Damn," Rudolph said.

"Tell me about it," I said back.

11 INVESTIGATION

The very next day I woke up and headed straight downstairs, to find out that school had been canceled for the rest of the week, due to the events that transpired during the election. I guessed that the news was not going to go into detail about what happened that night. I walked over to the living room and turned on the TV, switching it to the news network. The news was going to be on around seven, which meant I had about an hour until it aired. I walked back to the kitchen and grabbed a glass of water and sat it down on the table for later.

I walked back upstairs and walked into the bathroom, looking into the mirror. My face was pale and my eyes were bloodshot. I washed my face and decided to shave. I grabbed my straight blade and started going. When I was about done, I heard a knock at the door. *Ugh.* I started to walk away from the bathroom and back downstairs to open the door. It was Ulysses; he had the newspaper from downtown.

"Hey, what brings you here this early?" I asked.

"The local news has already caught wind of what happened last night, and as of right now, the State Police are investigating. Other news stations are already here and are at the Central Police Department, asking questions about what is going on," he said, as he walked in and passed me to the kitchen, leaning on the table.

I closed the door and walked towards him, "With the State Police investigating, it's bound to reach the Commonwealth, and we all know that they're going to send their investigators too. I am hoping that the evening news has it covered, and afterwards, we can go get the others and talk about everything," I said.

"Why don't we go to Sean's house first and start to round everyone up and check out the town? We can scope out the courthouse and possibly the police station. Go get ready," Ulysses said.

"Okay then, give me a few minutes."

I walked back upstairs and went into my room to get ready. I put on a shirt and changed my pants, into shorts, and went into the bathroom to double-check that I shaved everything off of my face before heading back downstairs.

"We should at least wait a few minutes; I want to see what is going on for today's news," I said.

"Sure, why not. It's early anyway," Ulysses responded.

We both sat on the couch and waited, as the news started, beginning with a brief intro about everything they were going to cover in the next hour. But of course, they started with the weather, then cut to a commercial.

"They have to get to the time sensitive stuff soon! I hate commercials! They should've covered the important stuff first, then the unimportant. Don't get me wrong, the weather is important, but not today, even though right now it's 50 degrees," Ulysses said.

"It doesn't matter," I said.

We sat and waited for them to come back on the air. Ulysses was still sitting too close to me, which didn't bother me. It is always good to know that someone is nearby. I moved a little bit, to give myself breathing room, when the news finally came back on.

"Today's election turned scandal, in the town of Dutchville, where voter fraud has shaken up the School Board, Sheriff, and even the Mayor elections. The Mayor of Dutchville is in custody for aiding with voting fraud, and many believe that the mafia, under control of a local Italian businessman, orchestrated the entire operation. Schools will be closed for the rest of the week, until Monday the 23rd. The Local, State, and Sheriff's officials are all investigating this issue, and it is possible that the governor will send out his attorney general investigators to look into this," the reporter announced.

"Celina, our field reporter, is out in the County of Pikerland, at the local police station with Sheriff Ray, the County Sheriff and the lead investigator," the other news reporter said.

The screen switched to Celina, with Sheriff Ray outside of the downtown police station and other reporters nearby.

"Good morning everyone. I am here with Sheriff Ray, the County Sheriff for Pikerland County. He is the arresting officer of Mayor Larry McCreedy, Mayor of Dutchville. What do you have to say about the current situation?" Celina asked.

"Well, I have been investigating the suspected mafia for about two years, until Mayor McCreedy asked me to back off. Then after a solid lead came to my office in Adamstown, I picked up where I left off, this time, with a real chance of catching them. The mayor tried to stop us, until we found proof that he was in on the fraud too. Then we had him," Ray said.

"What did it feel like when you were told that there was, in fact, a mafia working in the town?" she asked.

"At first I was really angry, especially since my investigation got shut down. But when I found out that the mayor was involved, it all made sense," he said.

"What do you think the outcome will be?" Celina asked.

"Hopefully, these people will be locked up for a long time and an ugly weight will be lifted from this town," Ray said.

"Back to you at the station," Celina announced.

"I wonder why they didn't say anything about the FBI being there too? Like when the FBI shows up, you know it's bad," I said.

"My guess is that Wallace hasn't called in to report

his findings. We should get going now. They're not going to talk about anything important for the remainder of the time," Ulysses said.

We got up from the couch and started to walk to the door. I opened the door and let Ulysses go out first. Then I closed the door behind me, locking it to be safe. I walked over to the sidewalk, and we made our way to Sean's house.

"At least the weather is nice," I said. "It's great to be able to wear shorts."

"Really, you wear shorts all season long. You always say that it's summer somewhere on Earth," Ulysses remarked.

"It's true. It's always warm somewhere," I said.

We were about two houses away from Sean's house, and we heard someone approaching us from behind, running at a fast pace. I turned around to see who it was. but it was too late. They tackled me the ground and onto the hard concrete sidewalk.

"What is wrong with you Rudolph?!? You are such an asshole! You could have really hurt him!" Ulysses yelled.

"I had to get back at him for yesterday! Calm down...he looks fine to me," Rudolph said.

I got back on my feet and looked at the both of them, "Okay, don't flip out Ulysses…but I think some of my ribs are busted…damn it!"

"Dude…" Rudolph started, as he followed us to Sean's house. I hobbled along, with the help of Ulysses.

"Are you sure you still want to go?" Ulysses asked.

"Yeah…I'm fine…I just need some ice."

We finished our walk down the sidewalk and walked into Sean's yard, to get to his front door. Ulysses knocks on the door, as I held my chest in pain.

Sean opened the door and kept it open, walking away and signaling us to enter, without saying a word to us.

"What happened to you this time, Mr. I Fall Down the Stairs on the Regular…did you fall again?" Sean asked.

"No, smart ass. Rudolph attacked me a couple of minutes ago, and I think he broke a couple of my ribs. I can feel the slight gaps. Do you have ice to give me?" I asked.

"I do…it's in the freezer. I'll get it. In the meantime, we need to talk about what all of this means, for us, and for the future of our school," Sean said, walking away from the living room and into the kitchen.

"Yeah, you'll need to set the student body at ease, let them know that this won't affect our elections. Assure them there will not be any fraudulent voting at our school," Rudolph said.

"Basically, our party will be the majority, but they will need to run school board elections again. This is going to be a very strange rest of the year," I said.

"Here's the ice...I hope it helps out. So, what we can do about this whole investigation," Sean asked me.

"Yeah, so now what?" Rudolph asked.

"We sit and wait until Sheriff Ray stops by or until Hazel updates us on what is going on at the Police station downtown. We need to figure out what is going to happen next," Ulysses announced.

"I think its kinda dumb that they canceled school over this. What is the worst that could have happened over there? Fights? That doesn't really happen that often," I said.

"Better to play it safe than sorry," Sean said.

"We should go out and maybe see Sheriff Ray and get any more information on what is going on, even though we know a lot right now. Wallace surprised us all that he works for the FBI...he must know more than all of us combined," I explained.

"Alright, fine. We'll go out and see Wallace...to see if we can get more info about this, or anything," Ulysses offered.

We started to get up and made our way out of Sean's house, to go back to my place so that we could drive downtown. I brought the ice pack with me, and we went on our way. As we left, I noticed an old-fashioned mustang driving towards us and then pulling into the Rossi household.

"What bullshit! They should be in jail right now! Did they let those bastards out on bail?!?" Sean shouted.

"This isn't good...go into the bushes so they don't see us, and wait until they go inside," Ulysses said.

We quickly got into the large bushes and sat there, and waiting for them to go inside. The whole gang was there, Leo, Stefano, Thomas, and James... all out on bail. Once they were inside, we quickly got inside of my house and locked the door, closing all of the curtains.

"If they're on bail, they can't do anything to us. They can't even go to school for a while," Ulysses said, trying to reassure us.

Sean hissed, "I don't like this. They know it was us, that we got them arrested...what if they come after us? They know where we all live and what we do."

"Don't worry. It's no big deal. They are probably on

house arrest. The police will know where they are at all times," Rudolph said.

"Well that's good," I said.

We sat in the dining room across from the kitchen in silence. It felt like forever until Sean broke the silence.

"We're just sitting here, doing nothing, while Harper is out somewhere doing god knows what," Sean said.

"He's out with some family, and he won't be back until tomorrow afternoon. He'll be fine without us," Ulysses said.

"It's best we stay in, until Sheriff Ray calls one of us or stops by to talk with us," I said to everyone.

"So, we sit locked up in your house until Sheriff Ray or Wallace calls us to come down to the station for our statements?" Rudolph asked.

"Basically. I refuse to go outside and get shot by one of those pricks."

"It's settled…we stay here until further notice," I said.

While everyone was still sitting in the dining room, I went upstairs and grabbed my phone from my desk, to tell my father about everything, including my ruined ribs. After that, I got a call from Sheriff Ray, telling me that he needed us at the station downtown. He wanted us to write our statement immediately, while all of the details were fresh. I walked back downstairs to tell the others. It was about ten o'clock, and the streets downtown were becoming more active.

"Hey, I just got a call from the Sheriff, and we need to get to the station right now to give our statements," I announced.

"Well, let's go. No time like the present," Ulysses said back, as he stood up and walked towards the door, with Rudolph and Sean.

We went outside and got into my car to drive downtown. With four people in the car, it was maxed out, and I couldn't drive very fast because of my ribs…and there was the matter of the absent seat belts. I was surprised that Ulysses even entered the vehicle, after saying it was too dangerous to ride in. Maybe he just wanted to get his interview over with.

"Your car isn't that bad after all…it's just…no seat belts, no airbag…but I'm guessing you don't care, especially since you drive it anywhere, regardless of the traffic," Ulysses commented.

I ignored Ulysses and focused on my drive downtown. People were giving us strange looks because of the age of the vehicle. Once we got near the outer edge of downtown, we soon realized that there were a lot more people at the police station than what we all expected. There were so many news agencies and private reports standing around, with others watching. We all got out and pushed past all of the people in our way. Luckily, no one hit my ribs.

"Great, you all made it here in one piece. We need to get to work immediately," Wallace said to us.

Wallace grabbed one of the detectives and told him to take us to the conference room, for our statements and additional questioning. We followed the detective across the building and into the room where Sheriff Ray was sitting. He was expecting us.

"Welcome boys. We should start with a quick update on what you guys missed after yesterday," Ray announced.

"Yeah, we have a lot of questions," Ulysses said.

"Sure," he said. "Alright...this morning the Rossis, and everyone else involved, were released on bail, and before you ask, that means the mayor too. But that doesn't stop us...we will be able to monitor their every move, and none of them took a plea deal. Since all of you helped out with the case, and it was your tip off that lead to the arrest, your testimony will be pivotal in sending them to jail. Wallace and I have a lot on them, but you boys are the key," Ray explained.

"What exactly are the charges going to be?" I asked.

"Crimes against property, fraud, blackmail, and bribery...possibly inchoate offenses, attempt, conspiracy, incitement, since we caught them early," Ray informed us. "Now here's the paper to write your statements on. Make them as detailed as possible. It will help out a lot, and you are free to go when you are done. I'll let you know if we hear more. Be safe out there, and report any suspicious activities from the Rossi residence. If they are planning to retaliate, you will probably be the first to know."

"Blackmail? Bribery?" Rudolph asked, confused.

"The Mayor claims that he was blackmailed into doing this and that the blackmail resulted in his refusal to accept a bribe. If that turns out to be true, he could walk away from this, a free man" Ray said.

After finishing our statements, we got up and left, setting our papers down so that Ray could get them. I was the first person out of the door, and I waited for everyone else to exit, so that we could go back home.

The drive home was very quiet, until we passed the Rossi house, where there were more cars there than before. I brushed it off as nothing...hoping it was just lawyers or more investigators.

12 MONDAY ATTIRE

The whole investigation was still underway after four days. Monday, the worst day of the week. I left my room to go downstairs and get my outfit for today: pink shorts, blue and white palm tree shirt, and rooster socks with red flats. I went back upstairs to the bathroom and took a shower and got dressed.

Once I finished, I made my way downstairs to make breakfast and check my bag, to make sure I had everything ready to go. Phone, tablet, binder, and algebra book ready. I had to go back upstairs to do my hair, and then I headed out for the day. My phone was 76%, which was fine. I didn't use it very often at school anyways, and if it died, I could always charge it at school during study hall. Today was supposed to be warmer than yesterday, so instead of driving to school, I chose the long route and decided to walk along with everyone else on the street. I saw Sean and Rudolph ahead of me, so I picked up my pace to catch up with them. Ulysses was probably already at school, as usual. He sure does love to bother teachers before school hours begin.

"So we all chose the shorts and flat shoes for Monday – we read each others minds," Sean said. "Even button up shirts with different colors."

"Graph paper shirt with red dots and blue, light blue shirt with seagulls for you Rudolph...we make the perfect summer wear for late November," I said to them. "We could make really bad models for men's fashion. If anyone asks us why we look like this, just say we are twinning."

We continued our way to school where more people were entering the building. We walked inside and made our way to the middle of the hallway, where Ulysses was at his locker already putting stuff in.

"You arrived early today again. You never seem to talk to us when we get to school," Sean said.

"I was wondering if Pete would drive his car, but I

guess not. Anyways, I come early because I like talking with Mr. Mickelson. Harper is around here somewhere. He went off to his class because he needs to talk with his teacher," Ulysses said.

"Don't forget to tell him that he needs to go to the police station to write his statement about what happened on Wednesday," I said.

"Baseball boots with shorts?!? What are you thinking?" Rudolph asked Ulysses.

"Look, I was busy, and I wanted to get here early," Ulysses explained.

"Whatever…hey, you over there…do you think we look good today or what?" Rudolph asked some girl.

"No, all of you think it's summer, and it's not…idiots," she said and walked away from us.

"Unnecessary," I said. "We need to get to our classes. Rudolph, we need to get to physics before eight."

Rudolph and I left the group, as we headed off to physics. We walked down the hallway and up the stairs. We heard some people talking about Wednesday and the news, which was everywhere. Apparently, our names were mentioned in the Sunday morning paper. I never read the paper, so I didn't know.

"Hey, you know you guys are in the news right now?

They said that you were there, right in the middle of it, when the police busted the mafia," Bill said. "What are you guys narcs or something?"

"Oh great, wonderful. Our names are out to the public. Nobody can do anything to us," I said back.

We continued our walk and finally got to Mr. Cannon's room, before eight o'clock. We took our usual seats and waited for him to enter the room.

"Good Monday morning to everyone. I want to make a very quick announcement about what happened on Wednesday and why the school was closed last week. To begin, there was a crime that occurred during the election, and some people were arrested, including Mayor McCreedy himself. You may have heard that on the news already, but there were also some students involved, and they will not be coming back to school. I know they were your classmates, but try not to worry about it. All of this will pass in time," Cannon announced.

"There were other students involved too. They were working with the Sheriff," Lisa said. "Pete, Sean, Ulysses, Harper, and Rudolph...they are still at school," she said, looking directly at us. "Why are they allowed to be here?" she asked.

"The Sheriff asked us some questions, and we answered them," I explained. "That's it...no big deal."

However, it clearly was a big deal. Everyone in class erupted with questions about that night and wanted to know more about it.

"Okay, okay, everyone quiet down. We need to get back to work. You can talk during your study halls and lunch period," Mr. Cannon said.

The class got quiet and started to work on school work for the rest of the period. In a way it was a relief. I wanted to tell more about what happened, but I decided that it would be better to give one speech to as many people as possible. Once class got out, Rudolph and I parted ways, going to our next classes. With college algebra up next, I was eager to talk to Sean, to see if anybody said anything to him. I also wondered if anybody was saying anything to Wilson. Even though we didn't spend a lot of time with him, he was still a good friend and was associated with our group.

There were a lot of people in the hallways, asking me questions about what happened. I had to ignore them...I had to be in class on time before Ms. Ray yelled at me.

Once I got to Mr. Ray's room I see Sean already

talking with Wilson about what happened.

"Hey, you made it, I already heard about everything, amazing!" Wilson said. "I can't believe you guys got them arrested."

"They won't be on the board ballot next week," I said.

"About that, what are we even going to do for meetings? Like I don't vote I'm just a historian, but its just going to be one party control of the school?" Sean asked.

"Acting like an oligarchy for the rest of the school years doesn't sound that bad, or we can set it up as the Roman Republic, have Jack and Adam be the consuls and have students be the Senate. They can be shuffled out every month and only if you want to do it," I said.

"What about you?" Sean asked.

"I might resign, I already know that if we do that I'm going to be removed from office, after busting those guys you might want to consider it too," I say. "We are going to become very unpopular with almost two-thirds of the school, especially the seniors."

"I was going to be removed anyway, look at me, no one likes me," Sean says.

"Maybe because you're always mean to some people," Wilson chimed in.

"I know but being the meanest friends show that I'm the one who cares the most out of the rest," Sean said.

"That is true but...let's say you make a lot of enemies on the way of doing that," Wilson said.

"Maybe during lunchtime, I'll go tell Jack and Adam that you should run the board like the Roman Republic and that I'm going to resign when I get to Geography class. They will understand why," I said.

"I might as well tell him during study hall if he's not proctoring for the ninth and tenth graders," Sean said. "I'll be in his room during study hall, you should join me along with Ulysses."

"I'll tell him when I get to health class," I said.

"Sorry for being late again, I was talking to some teacher about what was going on last week on election day, I can assure all of you know what happened," Ms. Ray announced.

"What are we doing today?" I asked.

"We are going to work on imaginary numbers, those things back in Algebra Two that no one liked," Ray said smiling.

"Well great, I hated those things back then," Wilson said.

Ray proceeds to pass out the worksheet on what we

are going to work on, this was going to be hard. I always tell myself math is my strongest but some days that leaves the brain.

"You have until Wednesday to complete this," Ray said.

"I'm going to need some serious help with this," Wilson said.

"Don't worry if we go slow and check out work with this stupid *i's* we will get it done and done the right way," Sean said.

"Today is not my day for math, but math is important and I have to do it, it's only fifteen questions," I said.

"I swear this is a joke," Wilson complained.

"Just stop complaining and do it," Sean said.

—

After working on this mad paper with crazy characters in it class was finally over and I could go to boring health class and tell Ulysses what the plan is for the rest of the year.

"I'll see you in Mickelson's room after health class," Sean said walking away.

I walk down the hall and the stairs to reach the health room, I see Ulysses waiting by the door looking into the class that is about to leave, looking through the window I can see Mrs. Lurgo talking to the class still and I can tell all of them are not happy since they're about to be late for the next class.

"She still keeps talking in there," I said.

"Yeah," Ulysses chuckled.

"Sean likes her because she talks a lot and I don't know why though," I said.

Mrs. Lurgo lets everyone leave and they all rush out, we are the first ones to enter the room and take out seats. Everyone got into the room and settled down the empty seats from Stefano and James.

"Sean and I talked out the future of the student board and the both of us are planning on resigning from the board and have hopes that they create the Roman Republic since it's a one-party control for the rest of the year," I said.

"Really? Why is that?" Ulysses asked.

"I believe the both of us are going to be voted out of office after what happened over the last couple of days, if I go you're coming with me," I said.

"I have a doctors appointment in ten minutes, so the class is going to be canceled, sorry, but there will be a sub coming in soon," Mrs. Lurgo announced.

"Great," Ulysses said.

"I don't get her, why even come to school when you need to leave early?" I asked. "Just come in late."

"It doesn't matter to me, we get a free day from here again," Ulysses says. "It's not like this work is important after all."

"Duh, it's health all we learn about is drugs and reproductive cycle and that's it," I said.

"Do we have to go to court to testify against them? If we do that's going to be wonderful, the town citizens vs the mafia in town," Ulysses says.

"Yes we do, we might want to gather up after school and see Sheriff Ray about that, he's most likely going to be at the central police station in town and not in Adamstown so you don't have to worry about riding in my car," I said.

"I find it amazing that we are going to testify against our own town Mayor because of this," Ulysses said.

"He's greedy and this is what happens to him, jail," I said.

"They all got served, we couldn't have done it without Hazel," Ulysses said.

"She just told me that it was all true even though I didn't believe all of you in the first place," I said.

"Sometimes the source is the only way to get

someone to listen, we don't work for the mafia and I get it you wouldn't believe us because we like to joke around," Ulysses said.

"I want to know why and how they even got off on bail, like come one they're mafia members, a flight risk at the lease," I said.

"They could have given up their passports that that's it, but it is suspicious," Ulysses said.

"It doesn't matter, they have to be home and not break any more laws from here to the courtroom, seems easy enough for them," I said.

13 BUMPING OFF

Ulysses and I got out of health class and headed upstairs for study hall, while the freshmen and sophomores had lunch together. Everyone except for Harper was in Mr. Mickelson's room talking about politics, while he was away monitoring lunch. As we walked in, I saw Sean and Rudolph already sitting on Mr. Mickelson's couch.

"Where is Harper?" Sean asked.

"He probably went to talk to Mr. Mickelson," I answered.

"I say good luck to him dealing with the underclassmen downstairs, Mickelson is proctoring lunch for those fools, have you seen lately that they fight among each other like gorillas," Sean said.

"Over what? It's not like they have priorities in life," Ulysses said.

"They fight because of what they say, they think they lead the school, girls, and they fight the seniors because they're adults can can't fight back without bad things happening to them," Sean said.

"Girls I get it, but they think they run the school it's a joke. They need more time until they even run the school," Ulysses said.

"Fighting the seniors is a death sentence, for the both of them, one gets arrested and the other gets fucked up, simple as that," Rudolph chimed in.

"Well, they're going to learn someday to gets themselves together, if not, I don't know what could have to them," I said.

"Anyways, we got our report cards for the marking period, they're on his desk over there," Rudolph said.

"Great, I want to see what I got for the year so far," Sean said.

"Same, I think doing pretty good this year so far," I said walking to Mickelson's desk.

I start to pass out the reports card for everyone.

"Let's see here...normal grades, as usual, I already saw

yours passing them out we're all good," I said.

"First marking period is the easiest, second is going to get worst followed by the next and the next," Ulysses said.

"After the first semester things get really slow," Sean said.

"As long as you pass that's all that matters, numbers shouldn't control you, no one in today's time is going to tell you something by memory unless you have no sources to help you," Rudolph said.

"Yeah...what he said," I said.

"Anything good in the world of politics other than what is going on?" Ulysses asked.

"I haven't checked. I think something is going down in Washington," Sean said. "Something over immigration as usual I believe."

"Always that issues and health care, real problems are taxes and jobs, I get health care but who really cares?" Ulysses said.

"Health care is important it's just...we have bad policies on it, think like other countries, free health care," Sean said.

"Americans don't want free health care, we are entitled to pay because we believe that the more we pay the better the service will be," Rudolph said.

"Education is important too," I said. "No education means none of these can be done."

"Uneducated white people do seem to be on the rise lately," Ulysses said.

"Some political parties rely on uneducated people to win races and the smart get served because of it. Smart equals dangerous apparently," Sean said.

"Well, you have a smart mouth after all," Ulysses said.

"I don't care I have gotten this far and lived," Sean said.

"Stop bickering, we can continue the federal politics after school. In the meantime we need to attempt the Red Party before we part ways," I said.

"Since I'm Pete's clerk I'm forced to give up my seat when he leaves," Ulysses said.

"See what happens when you run for an office seat? Bad things can happen just like this and what went down last week," Rudolph said.

"It's over for us, where are the resignation papers?" Ulysses asked.

"They're over at his desk, it might be inside where it could be locked so we need to see him to unlock it," I said.

"Why leave when the party needs you in this time of need? You can't leave Jack and Adam hanging," Rudolph said.

"Tomorrow I'm going to speak with them about what is going to happen, I think they'll understand the situation, the school government is going to change into a Roman-like Republic-Democracy, every student votes and they get to decided on the votes if its worthy enough to be passed," I explained.

"I see nothing wrong in that," Ulysses said.

"So...what are we going to do in study hall? It's just us in here. We should go online and see if there have been any updates from the police. The FBI has to be getting here by now...it's been four days," I said.

"Yeah, let's do that," Sean agreed.

We pulled out our phones and started to look up the local and state news, but we were having issues...no signal in the area.

"Why isn't there a signal?!? We always have a signal in this building! Maybe if I move closer to the windows..." I said. "Are you having the same issue I am?"

"Yes, I am," Sean said.

"Do you think we should call the main office, see if

they know what's up?" Ulysses asked.

I walked over to the phone on Mr. Mickelson's desk and picked it up. I didn't hear anything, no dial tone at all, and when I tried to type the office number, it didn't work at all.

"The phones are dead," I said to them.

"What the fuck? What is going on here? Cell service gone, and now the landline phones are dead? Do you think someone could be playing with a phone jammer? Is it you Rudolph?" Sean asked angrily.

"No, I like a good joke, but not this,that's illegal to do," Rudolph said.

We weren't the only ones bothered by the interruption of service. We saw students walking out of their rooms and heading downstairs, but we decided to stay put until a teacher came back, not wanting to get in any trouble.

"You guys okay in here? I'm going to see if I can find out what's going on," Wilson said, as he entered the room.

"It's probably nothing. I'm guessing someone, probably a freshman, was messing with a phone jammer," Ulysses said to him.

Wilson walked out of the room leaving us alone.

With all that had happened, I was hoping for a coincidence. The ninth graders don't know better and do really stupid shit all the time. All freshmen are like that, they want to be at the top but can't, they have many years until that. A lot of students had made their way to the lower floors of the building, leaving the third floor eerily quiet.

"If we stay here, we don't run the risk of getting into trouble. But if something is going on..." Sean started, breaking the silence.

"Let's just stay here and wait it out. What can go wrong?" I said.

We walked away from Mickelson's desk and sat on the couch, waiting. I looked out the window, checking out the other side of the building. I saw someone running down the hallway, coming towards us.

"Hey look. It's Harper...running to get us," I told everyone.

"Why is he running? It's not like we're going anywhere," Sean said.

"Obviously, something's up," Rudolph said.

"Maybe..." I said.

Harper busted through the door and slammed it shut, looking petrified.

"What's wrong?" Ulysses asked Harper.

"Leo, Stefano, Thomas, and James are all here...in the cafeteria..."

"What do you mean? They are on bail and are not allowed to come to school ever again..." Sean stammered.

"Harper, why are they here?" I asked.

"They want us...they want to kill us...and they are threatening to kill everyone..."

"What do you mean?" Ulysses asks.

"They have guns...I ran," he said, still out of breath.

"Oh shit, we need to call the police right now!" I yelled.

"We can't...they must be the ones using the phone jammer, blocking all telecommunications in and out of the building," Rudolph said.

"We need to do something, right now. Nobody is up here. We have a better chance of getting out and calling the police," Ulysses said.

"That's going to take too long. There has to be another way," I said.

"I have an idea, but it's going to be risky," Harper said.
"Do it," I said.

Harper ran to the closest fire alarm and punched the

glass, pulling down the alarm handle.

"Why did you do that?" shouted Rudolph.

"The fire department will come...and the police. Anybody not in the cafeteria will leave. They'll know this isn't a drill," Ulysses answered.

About a minute passed with the fire alarm going, until the all of the power was cut, causing the lights to shut off...and the alarm.

"Shit...they must have gotten to the main power room," Harper said. "Hopefully the fire company got the call in and are on their way."

"We can't stay in here...they're going to find us and kill us. We need to leave, right now," Sean quavered.

"You're right," I said. "But where do we go? We don't know which way they are coming from."

"I say we go long and try for the second floor. It's our best bet. Stay low and keep an eye out for anyone and anything," Ulysses directed.

"Sounds good...let's go," Sean said, standing up and going for the door.

"What if they come up here with us? That's asking for trouble," Rudolph said.

"It's a risk everyone here is willing to make," I said. "Getting out of here is the top priority, no escape equals not survival."

"Even though the signal is out we know the police are going to get here anyways, it's just a matter of time," Ulysses said.

"Let's go before we die up here," Harper said.

Sean was the first person to leave the room and enter the hallway. We all followed made a left turn to go the stairs that are located on the other side, to make our way to the second floor.

14 THIRD FLOOR

As we walked down the hallway, slowly, we heard the commotion from the lower levels, and gunshots to go along with it. Scared, we took it slowly down the hall, making sure everyone stuck together. We looked into all of the classrooms that we passed, checking for other students. They were all empty.

"We should go inside some of these rooms...look for anything that we could use as weapons," Harper said.

"None of our teachers have weapons," Ulysses said. "We have the numbers for the time being."

"I know, but we can always find little things like rulers, books, anything we can throw, staplers and mugs, whatever will fit in your hands. Just keep your eyes peeled," Harper said.

I checked my phone again and saw that it still read, *no signal*. The time also said *12 o'clock*, and I knew that the passing minutes would feel like hours. Everyone was in a scared state, except for Sean and I. We tried to keep a cool and level head in this dangerous situation. The noises from the bottom floors started to quiet down, which meant that people were either dead or had escaped. I felt that we would be witness to both before we got out of there.

"Guys...what do we do, if we find someone who's been shot?" I said.

"Don't think about that...we need to just stay strong and get out of here. We can help anyone we come across, along the way," Rudolph responded.

"Those bastards! They go out of their way to shoot up a school because they get caught up in illegal activities...they should have never been left out on bail for this," Sean angrily said.

"It doesn't really matter why they are doing this... I just want to make it out of here," Rudolph said. "I want to make it to adulthood."

We had passed about eight rooms and looked into them through the windows, seeing nothing of value to help us. We passed the chemistry lab, and we decided to walk into there. Being a science room, we figured there had to be something useful inside of it.

"There must be chemicals in here," Sean said.

"Obviously...the bad thing is that none of us took chemistry, and mixing random stuff isn't going to help us right now, we could cause a leakage or even an explosion causing more harm to everyone," Ulysses said.

"Instead of standing here and talking about chemicals, we need to make a plan and escape from here," Harper said.

"Yeah, we should listen to Harper," Sean said.

"Then take it away, I'm all ears," Ulysses said.

"Okay, what we need to do is go out and make our way to the custodial rooms. We can break the mops and brooms to make stick weapons. Since they cut off the power, they can't see us on the cameras and don't know where we will be headed to," planned Harper.

"We cannot hide from this...we have to fight the battle here. We have the high ground after all, and we need to use it to our advantage," I said.

"If you can't beat them, arrange to have them beaten," Rudolph said to all of us.

We slowly opened the door back out into the hallway. We remained quiet, although the gunshots were loud enough to muffle any noise we were making. We kept going down the first hallway and made our way to the custodial room, to find the supplies we needed. We got in and soon realized that there was nothing in there at all, no mops or brooms, just an empty bucket.

"Who the fuck leaves their station unprepared for the work day?!? Check whose name is on the side," Sean said.

"Looks like it was Jake the janitor, aka, Wallace Vanschuster the FBI agent. He must have left his cleaning work at the courthouse on Wednesday night," I said.

"Well...dammit, he kinda fucked us over a little bit," Sean said.

"He didn't know this crazy shit would go down," Rudolph said.

"We can't sit in here for long! We need to keep moving and get to the second floor before they get up to us. They're still shooting, and we have to do something!" Ulysses said.

We left the janitor room and continued our way along the third floor, to get to the stairway. After the long walk, we finally turned and realized that there is a teacher's lounge on the floor. There were supplies in that room, in case of an emergency. We ran back down the other hallway to the teacher's lounge to enter into it.

"Damn! The door is locked," I said, attempting to open the door.

Harper pushed Rudolph and I aside, "I have this...move out of the way!" He kicked open the door, and the hinges on the top broke a little. We made our way in and saw screens in the corners, for the cameras that are located in the office. They were off, of course, but upon further inspection of the room, we found some things that we could use as weapons. We found some knives and a broom. Harper broke the broom into a stick. At the desk where the coffee maker was, there was a blue button that had the label, *In Case Of Emergency Press This Button,* at the bottom it also said, *EMERGENCY GENERATOR,* in white.

"Look at this! It's a button that will turn on the power! Why is it on the third floor here and not in the office?" I asked.

"Maybe because the generator is located on the roof of the building, and it might have been difficult to hard wire to the office," Ulysses said, walking towards the button. Plus if something happened to the office staff there is a back up just like right now."

"The bad thing is that it's locked and protected by the glass. We obviously don't have the key to unlock it," I said. "Mickelson probably has a key."

"Move...I have this," Rudolph said as he punched the glass with a mug. rushed to press the button, and the emergency lights came on. They were dim, but at least the electricity was restored. For how long? That was the question we all had in mind.

"We need to get to another room and press the Police call button, before they cut the backup power," Sean said.

We quickly ran out of the teacher's lounge and into the nearest classroom. Ulysses passed by me and jumped over the desk to reach the police call button, slamming it down to make sure it went off.

"There...we made the call without using a phone. Although it would be nice to call and talk to Sheriff Ray," Ulysses said.

With the police on their way for sure this time, we left the room and watched as the backup power got cut out, leaving us in darkness once again. The shooting still continued…we hoped that the flicker of lights gave the other students a sign that help was coming. We continued to walk back down the hallway, to recover some ground that was lost in backtracking to the teacher's lounge, in our successful mission to restore power long enough to call the police.

15 POLICE?

With the police on their way for sure, we are bound to be saved. We walked down the rest of the hallway and passed the corner, to make our way down the stairs. I looked at my phone once again and realized that the signal was back again.

"Hey look! The signal is back on again. We can call Sheriff Ray now and tell him that we are trapped in here," I said.

"Quick! Make the call, in case they turn it back off again," Harper said.

I quickly dialed Sheriff Ray's number and waited until he picked up the phone...he didn't. I left a voicemail, telling him what was going on and where the Rossi's could be at in the school shooting people.

"He didn't answer the phone but I left a voicemail telling him where we are and what is going on at the school. I hope he responds back," I said.

"He'll call back whenever he can. We need to keep moving for right now... we should search any other classrooms before we head down to the second floor," Ulysses said.

Alright, we should go in the computer lab and see if we can find anything else useful," Rudolph said, opening the door.

We all entered the room to find it empty again...*damn*. No one to help or to save...we needed more people to stop them. I closed the door behind me and locked the door, in case they came up.

"The gun shots have almost stopped. Hopefully, most of the students and staff must have escaped already," Sean said.

"Who could have managed to turn off the phone jammer?" Rudolph asked.

"I don't know, but whoever did it, we appreciate it so much," Ulysses said.

"We should stay here. The police are on their way right now, and we can't afford to get shot," Sean worried us all.

"Just take a deep breath...we are going to be okay, but we need to see if we can save others before it's too late or defeat them upfront since they want us. We can take them," Harper informed us.

As he finished his sentence, we heard the heart-racing police sirens in the distance, they were getting louder and closer each second. We all ran to the nearest window and looked out from it, seeing the local police about half a mile away from the school and some students running away from the building in horror.

"Wonderful, the police are finally here to help. I still don't trust the local police to even enter the building...by the sounds of the guns shots, there has to be more than five of them inside," I said. "They brought some backup with them.

"They have no escape from the school. They'll be shot or taken alive in cuffs. We need to get down from here to the police...they have to be coming up the stairs to the second floor by now," Harper said.

The police cars stopped a safe distance from the school and we could see all of the blue uniforms from the officers running to aid the students and staff that were already outside of the building.

"There is not many at all to take them all down...the state police have to arrive to help handle the situation. Even though this town is relatively big, there are only twenty-five officers plus the chief that patrols the streets...all of the rest are state officers," Sean said. "We are so fucked right now."

"Yes, yes we're fucked," Rudolph calmly said. "Now they know someone must have turned off their phone jammer for sure."

"With the State Police at least five minutes out, we need to keep moving to locate any more survivors," Harper said, walking to the door.

"There could be a hostage situation going on downstairs to prevent the police from entering in quickly. Trust me, these people are terrorists," Ulysses said, leaving the room.

"Come on guys...we are almost on the second floor and out of here. But I'm afraid of what we might see," Sean worried again.

"I don't think they even made it to the second floor before the police arrived. By now, they have to be more worried about the police now than us, for the moment," Ulysses reassured Sean.

"Most school shooters will run from the police because they are weak inside and know school's are defenseless from them making it an easy target, pathetic. This is the exception, they give no fucks," I said.

With only about thirty feet between us and the doors that lead to the stairs, we were hoping to make it downstairs without anymore shooting sounds, but we were sadly mistaken. When heard more shooting from outside. It sounded like a battle, with the law on one side and the criminals on the other and we were on the wrong end, risking our lives to get to the first floor. The very people who aimed to save us could end up shooting us all dead.

"Man, I hope they are doing okay out there. I don't want to see a police officer get shot and killed trying to do their job," Sean said.

"Don't worry, they have enough cover to protect themselves," Ulysses said. "They have the numbers to take them."

We opened the door to the stairway and slowly went down the stairs, trying not to create any noise in the process. We were afraid there might be more people working with them on the second level, and we wanted to make sure no one was on it. Once we finished making our way down the stairs, we opened the other door, and I made sure the door was closed behind me. Down another level, and the danger level increased by two hundred percent.

"We are now on the second floor, more dangerous, but we can do it. Let's search every room for students and staff in the meantime," Ulysses said to all of us, standing and waiting for what was to come.

16 NEW MEMBER

We started walking down the hallway going into the first room we saw, which was ironically the bathroom. We made sure that no one was inside of the stalls. It was the girl's bathroom, and it felt a little wrong going, but it didn't matter, with nothing but chaos and carnage going on below.

"I never knew that these bathrooms were so clean," Rudolph said.

"Keep moving…we need to get to the next room over to find anyone," Harper said.

We left the restroom and went into the second room, which was the Civics classroom. The door was locked, and the room lights were off. Harper as usual kicks open the door and the door swings open with ease. The room was dark and quiet. The shooting had also calmed down for the time being, and we went to the window to see through the courtyard and track field.

"Would you look at that...there they are...with hostages," Sean said.

"This keeps getting worse by the second...they have hostages and want us dead too. They are going to hold out for as long as possible," Ulysses said.

"With them downstairs, going to the first floor is insta-death for anyone. I can bet they have at least twenty people helping them that we don't know of or even more," I said.

With that in mind, we left the room and continued the walk on the second floor. Pulling the fire alarm must have gotten more people out of the building, quicker than we all expected. We were ready to find anyone, to protect them when the time came. Before we hit the corner of the building, we heard a noise coming from the men's bathroom.

"Do you hear that?" Rudolph asked.

"Yes, someone's in the bathroom. We should go and see who," I said.

"Whoever it is, they are obviously not a member of

the mafia because we all saw them on the lower levels," Harper said.

"What we need to do is go in and find out. I'll go first, then Harper behind me as cover, just in case they fight back," Ulysses planned.

Harper and Ulysses snuck into the bathroom to see who it was. Once they got in there, we could hear a loud, *Oh Shit!*, and a stall slamming. The rest of us ran in, to their aid if needed.

"It's me...Wilson, the guy from College Algebra," a familiar voice said. "Chill out, okay. Those guys downstairs really fucked me up."

"What did they do to you?" Rudolph asked.

"They shot me in the shoulder...it hurts like hell. I came up here because I thought no one would be up here to hear or see me...I thought you guys were already out or dead because it was our lunch time when this shit happened."

"No, we were up in Mr. Mickelson's room talking about the investigation when it started. Harper was downstairs with Mickelson when the shooting began," Ulysses said.

Wilson was fixing his shirts and washing the rest of the blood off of him, "About Mr. Mickelson...he was taken captive by Leo and the other assholes who are doing this, at least fifteen of them, most we don't know who."

"Do you know anyone else taken as hostages?" I asked.

"Yes, I was taken as one too because Thomas still has beef with me after the fight last week. He wanted to kill me then and there...Ms. Ray is also one of them and so is Dr. Chevalier. The office staff is gone, and so are the TV's. It looked like World War II was happening inside our building. So many people got hit...the fire alarm made it worse, but more people got out in a matter of minutes," Wilson stated.

"Damn! It seemed like a good idea to do that...we were hoping it would trigger an auto call to the fire department and get everyone out," Harper said.

"Don't worry about it...you didn't know. We didn't know it would have been a bad idea to that...I would've done the same," Sean said.

We helped Wilson onto the counter by the sinks and tried to help him with the bleeding, as he told us what was going on downstairs. When we did that, we heard more sirens in the distance. I decided to take it upon myself to see who was coming. I figured it had to be the State Police or even Sheriff Ray. I got up to the window and took a look. The classic nearly all white cruiser of the State Police was the best thing I had seen all day. At first, it was one cruiser, then another and another. Each of them had partners and assault weapons to aid them. I also saw, in the foggy distance, Sheriff Ray's car, speeding down the road with what looked like Wallace in the passenger seat. I quickly grabbed my phone and called his number. Once he was out of the car he answered and quickly ran to see the Chief of Dutchville Police. Sheriff Ray is now officially in charge of what is going on now.

"Hello...where are you?!? Please tell me you guys are okay?" Ray asked.

"No, we are still trapped in the building. We found one person that got away from them, Wilson, but he's been shot in the shoulder and is bleeding as we speak. The others are trying to help him as much as possible. They have hostages, Mr. Mickelson, Ms. Ray, Dr. Chevalier, to name a few, and maybe some students that couldn't quite make it. I can see you from the second-floor bathroom," I told him.

When I finished telling him who was still inside, according to Wilson, Sheriff Ray started to speak again.

"Shit...I need to get in there right now. My sister is

Ms. Ray, and I can't let her get hurt by those fuckers...I have to go right now!" Sheriff Ray yelled and hung up the phone.

Fuck! I should have known that Ms. Ray was related to Sheriff Ray. I ran back into the bathroom to tell the others that State and Sheriff's Office were both at the school.

"Guys, good news...the State Police are finally here and so is Sheriff Ray and FBI agent Wallace. But the bad news is the hostages...Ms. Ray is Sheriff Ray's sister," I announced.

"Now we have to save them no matter what. Sheriff Ray has helped us with so much in the past week, we have to repay him. I say we go to the first floor and try to take them by surprise," said Ulysses.

"Impossible...they will kill the hostages if anybody tries to come near them. They didn't want things to go down this quickly. I was able to take out their phone jammer, when I made my escape, that's how I got a bullet in the shoulder," Wilson said.

"Without that, we would never have been able to notify Ray about the hostage situation," Harper said. "You saved us and the hostages by warning them before they get executed."

17 DANGEROUS PLAY

They were here on the second floor with us...I could hear them through the walls. How could they get automatic weaponry without being stopped? That was one of the first things we would have to go to the State and Congress about, when the hell was all over for everyone. We stayed in the bathroom for a little bit...they were searching the rooms for us and anyone who stood in the way. I could hear Ulysses breathing heavily, right beside me. Wilson was still sitting on the toilet – his face was pale, and his orange shirt was covered in blood...his and possibly others. My hand was covered in blood from his wound. We managed to stop the bleeding for a little bit, but we just needed to be quiet.

"They're right on the other side of the hallway," Sean whispered.

I tried to take deep breaths to calm myself down, but my ribs hurt like hell because we were sitting. I stood up and helped Wilson from the toilet seat.

"What are you doing? We need to lay low," Rudolph aggressively whispered to Wilson and me.

"I'm not staying in here to be executed by teenagers," I said back.

"Dude, shut the fuck up! We're going to get caught if you get any louder," Ulysses said.

"I could give two shits about it! If you don't come with me, you are a goner...follow me, and we might escape," I said.

Harper and Sean got up from the floor. Harper grabbed Ulysses and forced him to follow us. I knew he thought that staying in a room was best, but if they found us, we would have been easy, sitting targets. Rudolph was already peeking out the door to make sure no one was coming.

"Since we're at the center point on the second floor, there are a lot of blind spots on both sides. We don't know which way they could come from.... the left or the right side...," Rudolph said.

"We should head back up the stairs and try to get on top of the roof and hope for a helicopter to get us from there," Ulysses said.

"We need to go...I think they are getting closer to us," Harper said, the first to walk out of the door.

Sean was the last person to walk out of the bathroom and kept watch from behind, to warn us if they were coming. I was helping Wilson walk, and so was Rudolph. Ulysses and Harper stayed in front. From the corner and back to the stairway, we had to cover about twelve classrooms, about sixty feet. Those sixty feet would be slow to trek, but that no longer mattered. We heard the Rossis from the side and knew we were screwed.

"There they are! Shoot them, quick!" Stefano yelled.

"Fuck! Run, right now!" I yelled at everyone.

I let go of Wilson, who managed to get up with the rest of us in the run to the stairway. Sean, on the other hand, was the shortest member of our group and fell behind. I was so afraid that he would be shot next. The shooting increased, and they started to run after us. I could now hear Leo and his powerful M1911 shooting, but this time, he didn't miss Sean and me. I saw Sean get hit in the lower left side of his back, and he tripped and fell on the ground.

"Fuck, I'm hit! Pete, get me back up!" Sean yelled.

I ran back to get Sean off of the ground, taking a .45 ACP bullet straight to the left shoulder. I quickly got Sean back up on his feet, and we ran to the stairway. With the adrenaline high, I couldn't feel my pain yet and kept running. Sean took another pistol round in his right shoulder, trying to shield me from the bullets, but he stayed on his feet the whole time.

"Keep going…leave us behind if you need to. We WILL make it up there. Don't worry about us," I yelled at them.

The rest of them got to the stairway, unharmed. The bullets were flying past us, hitting the doors and glass. You could hear the magazines from the guns hitting the floor and them reloading. We made it to the doors for the stairs and quickly opened the doors then closed them. Harper was still there… he said nothing and locked the door, using the stick from the mop to block the door from being forcibly opened.

"This won't hold them for long, but it will give us enough time to hide in a room. Go, quick," Harper said.

Harper grabbed Sean and we walked up the stairs, meeting the rest on the third floor. Their faces were all pale. Rudolph was turning green and nearly vomited from seeing the blood.

"We need to hide quickly before they get up here! Quick, go to the other side where the roof stairs are," Ulysses said.

"We need to hide for a second, so we can tend to Sean. He's bleeding out…," Harper said.

The other bathroom was only about a few feet from where we were, and we all rushed in, taking the paper towels from the dispenser and toilet paper. First, we covered Sean who had the most injuries. I could wait…it was only a flesh wound, as far as I knew.

There we were…six students trapped on the third floor of our school. Half of us were injured by gunfire, and the other three were trying their best to help out with the wounds…but we are no doctors. We are just kids who go to school and were unlucky enough to be trapped in a nightmare. Between the roof and the mafia below us…there was no escape from there.

"We need to go now. I can hear them trying to open the door," Wilson said. "It's only a matter of time before they get in."

We got up and started to jog down the hallway and turned the corner. Harper pulled open some doors to make it look like we were inside, and Ulysses ripped anything off the walls that could stop them or help us in some way. Sean's bleeding started to stop, and mine was under control. Wilson carried Sean, with me to pick up the pace.

"We are almost at the turn...hurry..." Harper got cut off by the sound of a shotgun going off on the door and loud footsteps running up the stairs. "They're here, RUN!" He yelled.

There wasn't much we could do and some of us were injured but I had one thing up my sleeve, my phone's emergency service. I grabbed my phone from my right pocket and pressed the power button three times. The auto call for the police started, making an ear-piercing noise. I threw it in one of the rooms and continued on the way to the roof, hoping that the phone would distract them, buying us some precious time. When we got to the dead end, the door to the roof was being forcibly opened from the outside.

18 LAW HAS ARRIVED

Sheriff Ray and Wallace were there. The door burst open, and there they were…they must-have climbed the ladder to get on the roof.

"Are you guys okay?" Ray asked.

"Not even close…they're on the third floor with us and Sean, Wilson, and I are injured. Sean has the worst of the injuries," I hurriedly explained.

"Here, take these, some bandages," Wallace said.

He handed over the bandages and Ulysses took them to stop Sean's bleeding.

"You know after getting shot twice, it doesn't hurt as much…adrenaline is the best, right?" Sean commented.

The reunion was cut short by gunfire, once again, but closer. Ray pulled his gun out, at the ready, and waited until they turned the corner. The first person who rounded the corner was Thomas, with a shotgun. He took a shot at us, but Sheriff Ray started to fire before he could hit him twice in the legs, making him fall to the ground. Luckily, he missed all of us. Leo turned and Wallace shot at him, missing, but Leo took Thomas and got him up quickly. They ran away from us.

"Now they know we are here…we need to get the pressure on them to get them to surrender," Wallace yelled.

"They're not going to stop…they want us all dead!" Wilson shouted.

"The six of you stay behind me. Wallace, you and I are in front to protect them until we get down to the first floor," Ray said.

Ray had an assault rifle. Wallace carried a pistol and had a vest on that was labeled, *FBI* in yellow, with regular clothing underneath. He had not been prepared for this day. Ray was in full uniform and was ready for anything like any law enforcer.

"Why don't you use the rifle instead of your pistol? It

would kill them quicker," Sean slowly said.

"I can't risk lowering my gun and getting it while they're still on the third floor," Ray said.

We slowly walked behind Ray and Wallace. The three of us were all hurting from our wounds, and I was afraid that Sean was dying, slowly...I was afraid I was too. Wilson was doing better now. The other three helped us to move better.

"What's that noise coming from that room over there?" Wallace asked, pointing into a room.

"That's my phone's emergency call sound. It must have distracted them for a little bit before you could get inside," I explained.

Walking into the room, I reached for my phone, dealing with the extreme pain from my ribs and the gunshot wound. I turned off the alarm and walked back to the group.

"Alright now...the third floor seems secure. We need to head down to the next floor and fight them off from there," Wallace said.

"Why aren't the rest of the police coming into the school?" Ulysses asked.

"Yes, but the first responding officers saw the Rossis placing suspicious items near the door, and they have more powerful weaponry than the police," Ray said.

"You guys seem really unprepared," Wilson said.

"Son, you are never prepared for a thing like this," Ray answered.

We went past the other corner to the final side of the hallway, where the stairs were located. There was a trail of blood from there to the stairs. This indeed was hell itself, from zero to one hundred in a matter of an hour, injuries and police...we all knew that once we got to the second floor, they would be waiting for us. We had to be cautious and listen to the authorities.

Wallace and Ray were the first to go down the steps, and we were right behind them. Once we saw the door for the second floor, we noticed it was gone, blown away by the gunfire.

"Get down quick! They are right there!" Wallace yelled.

The six of us ran back up the stairs a little, to avoid getting shot, while Ray and Wallace started to open fire on the men that were shooting back at them. During the firefight, Wallace was hit a couple of times in the torso and so was Ray, but they had their vests, so they were still able to protect us. In the exchange, they shot three of the attackers.

"They won't give up for nothing, nothing I tell you," Ulysses said.

When the three shooters fell to the ground, motionless, we went back to see Ray and Wallace walking down the hallway. Ray had his assault rifle in his hands and his pistol back in his holster.

"The second floor is not secure yet...we need to keep moving before more come up," I said.

"I don't know about you guys but I feel really sick and I don't want to move anymore for a little bit...I just need to sit down," Sean said.

"You're right...I need to stop also. Can one of you stay, in case something happens?" I asked.

"You two stay...and Ulysses too. We'll keep going until we hit the first floor and try and secure it," Ray said, walking towards Ulysses. "Then we'll come back for you."

"I'll stay too...I can't leave them now," Rudolph said.

"Okay...Wilson and Harper, you two are with us...but make sure you stay behind. We take the lead...let's go," Wallace said.

With the four of them gone, it was just us, the wounded and those who decided to stay behind, so we wouldn't die alone. It was quiet...the shooting had subsided for a little bit, but I knew it would start up again.

"Try and stay awake for as long as you can. I'm going to go into the bathroom and get anything I can to help stop the bleeding," Ulysses said.

Ulysses ran down the hall and into the girl's bathroom, to get anything that would help us. Sean's graph paper shirt was now pink, covered in blood, and my shirt was now dark blue and still wet. The floor was painted with people's blood, evidence of the massacre that took place. Rudolph just sat there, staring into the distance, waiting for something to happen. Sean leaned on the wall, looking out the window, watching the police maneuvering with their heavy weapons. I looked outside too...I could see multiple ambulances out there, treating students and staff for injuries. It looked like a bomb went off...so many people looked hurt. In the back of my mind, I kept thinking about the aftermath of all of this and what the law makers have to say about it, sparking gun control once again and maybe doing something other than talking and talking and getting nothing done as usual.

"I'm back...take some of these and press them on the

wounds to clean them and slow the bleeding," Ulysses said.

"I don't want to hurt you, but it's the best I can do until you get fixed up," Rudolph said.

"Son of a bitch! That hurts like hell!" Sean weakly shouted.

"Don't worry about me...help him. Rudolph, check the janitor's closet, look for rubbing alcohol and anything we can use for more bandages...Sean's bleeding through all of these," I said, desperately.

Rudolph started to run away from us, trying to reach the janitor's office as quickly as possible. Ulysses, on the other hand, started to take off the bandages from Sean, covering the wounds with toilet paper. They got soaked quickly, making them seem ineffective to stop the blood, but the blood started to clot, finally slowing down.

19 BUSTED

The three of us stayed against the wall between the girl's bathroom and the first classroom on the second floor, which was another bathroom. Rudolph was on the other side looking for the janitor room to get cleaning supplies. The outside was hectic, police were scrambling, with more and more showing up, and we even heard a helicopter in the distance. The State Police had their SWAT forces out and ready for a breach and clear, once the highest-ranking officer gave them the go-ahead. By the looks of things, Sheriff Ray was definitely in command as an elected official for the county. He wasn't going to let them enter until he knew his sister was safe, as well as the other captured staff.

"They should hurry up and go in! They're going to let us die in here!" Sean yelled.

"No, they can't go in. The doors are rigged, and Ray is the only person that can tell them to enter. He wants to make sure his sister is safe before they go in," I explained.

"It's very quiet now...they might have apprehended the associates and others on the first floor," Ulysses said.

Ulysses stood up and moved right in front of us, blocking what was going on below.

"What we need to do is get Rudolph and go downstairs. They cleared this area for us and are on the first floor," Ulysses announced.

From the room right beside us, a person ran from out of the shadows, towards Ulysses, with a knife in hand, and he drove it right into his shoulder. Then he punched Ulysses in the jaw, knocking him out cold. It was Leo, the older twin! He was there, on the same floor as us. He pulled out his 1911 and pointed it at us.

"Both of you, stand up! You are coming with me, or I will unload my gun into the both of you!" Leo commanded.

"Alright, alright…stand up Sean, we need to listen to him," I said.

"What about Ulysses?" Sean asked.

"Forget him! I'm using the two of you to get out of here…now hurry!" Leo hissed.

We both stood up and walked in front of Leo. I looked over at Ulysses's motionless body, seeing blood go all over the floor and into his hair. *What fucking a mess this is, I said to myself.*

"In here…sit down! James, I have the important ones. Get on the radio and tell that asshole Sheriff that I have Pete and Sean. Ulysses is out cold in the hallway," Leo said.

"Alright, we should bring in the others, in case the Jew finds him in the hallway," James told Leo.

We were forced to sit in seats and watch, as Leo and James made their plans for what they were going to do with us.

"If you're going to shoot us, then do it! You're not going to make it out of here alive anyways," Sean said.

"Shut up! The both of you. You two are our ticket out of here…we say we have more hostages, and they will have to let us go free," Leo said.

"Hey, fuck face Sheriff!," James shouted into the radio.

"We have three kids on the second floor. One of them is bleeding from the back and is out in the hallway, not responding, and the other two are here with us. Better get a negotiator in here quick, or they leave in a box," James said.

"You're not making this any better for yourself...let them go, and we can find a peaceful end to this," Sheriff Ray said over the radio.

Leo took the radio and forced it near Sean's face. He pushed his thumb into one of Sean's wounds, making him scream.

"Do you hear that, *Sheriff?* I'm not fucking joking!"

"Ray, we're are stuck on the second floor, we-"

Leo looked at me and stabbed Sean, twisting it into his already wounded shoulder. Leo left it in the wound, as Sean started to cry.

"Now you know we're not fucking around. We get a way out of here, or else," Leo commanded, as he slowly put the radio down.

"Now we sit and wait until we hear back from him," James said.

"Why are you two even doing this? You're never going to get away with it! You need to surrender, or you're going to get shot by the police," I said.

"That's where you're wrong, ginger. We are taking the racist bitch with us, probably you too, and then we're going to the airport, until we get on a private plane out of the country. Then we're home free," Leo explained.

"Fuck you, greaser," Sean muttered.

"Shut the hell up," James said to Sean.

We started to hear shooting from the first floor. Ray and Wallace must have met some opposition on their way to the cafeteria, but we knew the focus was right here, on us, and not there. Sean started to compose himself and quieted down, while the two of them stood there, waiting for a word from the negotiator, and we sat in silence, waiting also.

"Why would your father even want to rig a school board election and the Mayor's election?" I asked. "It seems so petty."

"The whole scheme would have worked. The Mayor and my Dad are great friends. If he helped get the Mayor re-elected, he would help spread our business from New York to here, bringing in more members and spreading our influence deeper in America. He would hold an elected position as a board member and become popular with the town and student. Then he would run for Mayor. Once elected as the mayor, he would bring in more money for our family, get more companies established that secretly work for us," Leo explained. "But you ruined everything...so now we are going to kill you all." Leo stood there, staring at us, and James walked over to the door.

"He's gone!" James yelled.

"Where did he go?!?" Leo asked.

"He went into the bathroom...I can see the blood trail leading to it. I'll go take care of him," James said.

James ran out of the room and went straight to the bathroom, where Ulysses was. We were stuck in the room with Leo, helpless, and heard a loud gunshot from James's assault rifle.

20 PROMOSSO AL PADRINO

We all thought that Ulysses was dead for sure. We heard footsteps that were coming back to the room. Leo walked to the door and opened it, only to find Rudolph in the doorway. Rudolph grabbed Leo by the shirt and threw him to the ground. Leo tried to pull out his gun, but his hand was smashed by Rudolph's foot. The two started to fight, and Sean and I both watched as they fought for control. Rudolph stood nearly six inches higher than Leo, which made it easier to fight him, but Leo got the upper hand and kicked him away and onto the floor. Rudolph got up and faced Leo. Leo ran over to Sean and ripped out the switchblade that was left in him.

"You're not going to kill us today," Rudolph said.

"Watch me, Reindeer," Leo spit back.

Leo ran at Rudolph, knife in hand, and stabbed Rudolph in the chest, but after that blow, we heard two gunshots ring out from behind Rudolph. Leo fell to the ground, dead. He was hit the chest and neck, dying instantly.

"Don't worry...I killed James also. Let's get out of here," Ulysses said.

"I never knew you had it in you," Sean said.

"He drove that knife deep...he got a good stab in...I think he punctured the corner of my lung..." Rudolph said.

"It's almost over...Pete, take his 1911, and I'll take the knife, in case we run into any more of them," Ulysses said, dropping the rifle. "This assault rifle has no more ammo...it will be no use against them."

We left the room and went down the hallway, seeing more dead bodies. James body was hanging out of the girl's restroom, and blood was seeping out of it. I had the radio in my right hand and pulled it up to my face, to speak to whoever was on the other line.

"Weston, we killed them...James and Leo are both dead. Rudolph is hurt, and so is Ulysses. Rudolph has some broken ribs and a knife wound to the chest...we are heading down to the main floor as quickly as possible," I said over the radio.

"Shit! I hope you guys can stomach what happened down here...just meet us on the first floor, but don't wander too deep. It isn't secured...the cafeteria is still crawling with them. Wallace is trying to negotiate with them in the meantime," Ray stuttered, in disgust and fear.

We all knew that meant one thing...there was a lot of people dead downstairs. The mafia still had control on the first floor, and the cafeteria was their stronghold.

"I don't want to go down there...I refuse," Ulysses said.

"I don't want to either...it will scar us forever and haunt us," Rudolph said.

"We have to...it's the only way out of here," Sean said.

We walked slowly down the hallway, looking in every room again to make sure that no one was hiding, planning an ambush on us again. Some doors were closed, while others were opened. Each step was filled with horrible anticipation.

"Wait...there's stuff in the janitor's office...I saw it before. We need those supplies," Rudolph said.

We walked into the room. There was hydrogen peroxide and some cleaning rags on the table. Ulysses quickly opened the bottle and poured the liquid on the rag, putting it on Sean to stop his bleeding, and Rudolph grabbed another to put it on me. It hurt so much, but I knew it was only helping. After that, they bandaged themselves, and we headed on our way.

"I know that it was only temporary pain, but I hurt a little bit less now... thanks," Sean said to Ulysses, as we walked.

"Since Leo was their leader, since he's dead, would that mean that Stefano is now the leader?" Rudolph asked.

"Yes, according to Hazel. Once the leader is gone, the next one of them is promoted immediately and takes charge to retain order. Stefano has no clue his brother is dead yet," I said.

"He'll find out later, or not, if they end up killing him in a firefight downstairs," Ulysses said.

Once we got to the door that leads to the first floor, we knew that we were going to see the worst of our nightmares, but we were glad that all of us survived the gunfire and knife wounds. The first floor was like a giant maze, with some classrooms on one side and teacher rooms on other. It was the least simple floor plan, with many hallways, great for ambushes. Before we went down there, I wanted to see if Ray was in range of Stefano, to tell him that Leo was killed.

"Weston, if you are close to Stefano or Wallace, tell them that Leo was killed, and he's now the leader," I told Ray over the radio.

"Hey, Stefano, your bother is dead upstairs, along with James. It's up to you now – you can end this right now," Ray said to Stefano, with the rest of us listening too.

In response, we could hear shooting...and more shooting. Stefano was obviously not taking the news well.

"Let's just stay up here until they come and get us. They have to be giving soon," Rudolph said.

"Fine...let me tell Sheriff Ray," I said.

I told Ray over the radio, and he told us that they were going to let the hostages go, but we needed to back off, away from the glass door, where they would come out.

"They might let go of the hostages, which means once they are free, the SWAT team will storm in to get them," I said.

We sat and waited in the room that was closest to the stairway and waited for the hostages to make their way up, worrying about the door, since the door to the outside may have been rigged to explode. Mr. Mickelson, Ms. Ray, and Dr. Chevalier were the last ones left in the building, other than us, the students, police, and the mafia.

21 FIRE HAZARD

Negotiations seemed to take forever. Once they were released, the rest of the police would storm in to apprehend the suspects, on Sheriff Ray's orders. We sat in the room closest to the stairs and waited for the hostages to come up the stairs, where an evacuation helicopter was on its way that would take us to the hospital.

"We sit here and wait until all three of them are up here, then we get to the helicopter," Ulysses said.

"I can't believe that you killed another person..." Rudolph said.

"They were trying to kill us...I had to do something or I was going to die and the rest of you," Ulysses explained.

"You shouldn't feel bad about it – you had to do it," I said.

"Same...they deserved what they got," Sean agreed.

"We've been through so much...I'm starting to feel insane," Ulysses said.

I took a glance at my phone and saw that my dad texted me, asking if I was okay, what was going on an at school, and said he would get back to town immediately. I texted him what I could and said to meet me at the hospital in a few hours.

"Everyone, tell your parents what is going on. Also tell them to meet us at the hospital, once we get out of here," I said to everyone.

"My phone died...someone text my parents for me," Sean said.

"Alright," Ulysses said.

After taking some time to text our parents, we heard footsteps coming from the first floor. I opened the door to Ms. Ray, the mathematics teacher, the first out of three to be released.

"You made it, wonderful!" Sean exclaimed.

"It's horrible down there! I'm so grateful to be alive...Mr. Mickelson and Dr. Chevalier are still down there with them, still held at gunpoint," Ms. Ray said.

"Don't worry, your brother will get them out of this mess. Once we get the last two, we need to go upstairs and get to the chopper that is going to take us to the hospital," I explained.

"Once they're safe, the rest of the police are going to come in, and it will all be over," Ulysses said.

"Is there anything I can do to help...you're bleeding," she said.

"No, we are fine for now. There isn't much you can do to help us. The nurse's office is on the first floor, and we all agreed not to go down there," I said.

"Yeah, it's best to stay up here and wait. There is blood everywhere and death in the hallways and cafeteria...I can't unsee it," Ray said.

We sat and waited for any more people to come back upstairs and into our room. No one...it had been around ten minutes.

"What's taking them so fucking long to help us," Rudolph asked.

"I don't know really know right now-," I got interrupted by an explosion coming from the other side of the building. It was the State Police, making their presence known. They had enough of what was going on and wanted to end this shit right now.

"What was that?" Sean panted.

"It's the police...they're here to save us," Ulysses said.

"But the hostages, they are not secure yet...they are going to get them killed," Ms. Ray said.

"They know what they're doing, hopefully," I said. "I do not like that explosion though...the school might catch fire."

By then we could hear the helicopter getting closer to the school and making a landing on the roof, followed by shooting from where the cafeteria was located and loud footsteps, heading for the second floor. The door flew open, and we saw Wilson, Harper, Mr. Mickelson, and Dr. Chevalier storm into the room. Most of them had injuries and were struggling to move.

"Good...you're all here. We need to get out of here before the chopper leaves without us," Harper said.

"Ray said that the helicopter wasn't going to leave until he was on board, along with Wallace," I said. "Besides that, the police are now in the building in full force to take them out."

"Then we sit here and wait for them to make a return, but the building has sustained an explosion," Wilson said.

"The school might burn down, depending on what kind of explosion just happened. The police will take a minute to check every room before they go to the cafeteria, where the last stand is happening," I said.

"The building is going to burn the traps they had rigged to create a fire, so they could get out in a hurry," Dr. Chevalier said.

"In that case, we should start heading upstairs and wait until Sheriff Ray and Wallace get back up here," I said, standing up.

"We can't rush…most of us are injured rather badly," Harper said.

We left the room and started to walk down the hallway again. Harper was holding onto Sean, and Ulysses and Rudolph were holding me up. It was going to take some time before we got to the roof of the building. The shooting got more intense downstairs, and more officers were going in, leaving the road nearly empty. The helicopter on the roof got silent, to save gas. At least we hoped that it didn't leave because of the intense shooting.

Once we made the turn, we remembered that there were five dead people in the hallway, the three associates, James, and Leo, were all sprawled on the ground. *Good,* I told myself.

"How did they end up dying up here?" Harper asked.

"I shot them, both of them," Ulysses said.

I remembered that I had Leo's pistol and threw it down on the ground, so the police wouldn't shoot me, thinking I was one of them.

"You had to kill another person...I'm so sorry. It was self-defense against them," Ms. Ray said, reassuringly.

"Wait...I want to look outside and see what is going on in the courtyard," Mr. Mickelson said.

"Make it quick. We don't have a lot of time left," Harper said to him.

Mr. Mickelson ran into a room quickly and took a glance outside and run back in horror at what he saw.

"The building is on fire...we need to go, *right now,*" he said.

The fire was spreading, and we could only walk to the third floor to make our escape. The fire department was already there, with the rest of the emergency responders. We all hoped that Sheriff Ray and Wallace could make it back to us and escape, quickly and safely.

22 ESCAPE

We tried our hardest to pick up the pace to get out sooner, but all of us were in terrible pain and couldn't run like we used to, especially Sean, with two gunshot wounds and a knife wound. It was going to be extra close to our escape. We were halfway through the second floor when smoke started to come from the other side of the hallway, reaching us in a matter of seconds. The floor was getting slightly darker and harder to breathe in.

"We are almost on the third floor...we just need to keep going and ignore the smoke," Ulysses frantically said.

"Everyone just stay calm, and we can get out of here

alive. Someone, help me open the door for the rest of you," Dr. Chevalier said, pulling the door open.

Harper helped him out, and we slowly walked up the stairs. We made it to the third floor unharmed and had to deal with another long floor, until we got to the roof door and on the roof.

"Freedom is so close, I can feel it," Sean said.

"That's just the extra adrenaline helping you out again," Rudolph said.

"Jokes aside, we are going to make it," I said.

We heard more footsteps from behind us, and we turned to see Sheriff Ray and Wallace running towards us.

"You made it!" Ms. Ray shouted.

"We did, but we need to hurry! All of the perps are dead on the first floor, and the fire department is not going in until the place is secure. The State Police can deal with the rest of this god-awful mess," Sheriff Ray said.

"There was a huge firefight between us and they got a couple of officers hurt but they will be fine," Wallace said.

"I'm glad they all died…" Sean said.

"When we get to the hospital, I have to discuss

something about the mayor. It was something Leo told me when we were held captive," I said to Ray.

The school was heating up quickly, and we were getting tired from all of the walking around the building. The smoke was getting to us too. Another explosion from below rang out, and another. It must have been the doors getting heated up and activating the other bombs. We knew one thing, and it was that we had to escape as fast as we could before the flames reached us.

"Come on! We are only halfway through the hallway. We can make it to the heli," Sean said. "I can't wait till we get to the hospital!"

With no more opposition, I looked out the window to see the fire department make their way into the school to put out the fire.

"Hey, would you look at this! The fire department is finally entering the school to stop the fire from spreading," I said, pointing outside.

"I wonder what the state is going to say about this day…it's going to live in history," Mickelson said.

We went to Mr. Mickelson's room, and he went inside to get his bag and put something inside of it.

"Hurry up, Robert! The whole place is going turn to

ashes if you don't hurry it up!" Chevalier yelled.

"It was important! I'll explain later on, after we get to the hospital," Mickelson said.

We got up to the door that goes to the roof, and Ray and Wallace broke it open, to let everyone out before they left themselves.

"Hurry up! The roof won't be stable for much longer. We will take you to the hospital from here," the helicopter pilot said to us.

"Thank god you are here!" Sean shouted to them.

The two pilots guided us to the evacuation aircraft, and the healthy people that were left went in last. They closed the door, and we went off into the air, straight to the hospital.

"Thank you so much for saving us! We all owe you two something special when this is all over," Ms. Ray said to the pilots.

"Don't worry about it," the Captain of the helicopter said. "By the way, my name is Captain Wilks. And that over there is Jameson."

"Thanks, Captain Wilks and Jameson," I said.

The helicopter ride was very quick, and we got to the hospital in a matter of minutes. There were doctors and nurses on standby waiting for us. The helicopter landed, and the medical team got to work quickly, taking Sean and Wilson first since they were hurt more than the rest of us. I only had a knife wound and gun wound that barely even hit me, so I was going to be better off waiting than Sean. We were all messed up from the fighting. I knew they couldn't do anything about mine and Rudolph's ribs, but it didn't matter. We lived to see another day, unlike the mafia members. As soon as I got into the hospital, they put me right in the surgery ward. Apparently, Sean and I had the worst wounds, due to the switchblade. Nurse Grouse's husband was my surgeon.

"Don't worry, Pete. Your father is in the waiting room…you'll make it. You do need to undergo surgery, but you and your friends will live through this," Dr. Grouse said to me.

Then I went off to the ICU for my surgery. It felt like it was going to take them hours until they were done. With everyone out of the building and in the hospital, it didn't seem like there was anything left to fear.

23 AFTERMATH

"Monday, November 23, 2018, marks the deadliest school shooting in American History, with over 30 students, staff, and perpetrators killed, and over 70 people injured. The cause, a fraudulent school board election, which five eleventh graders brought to the attention of the authorities. The county Sheriff, Sheriff Ray, lead the sting that brought down the responsible mafia members. The massacre raises questions about gun control in the Commonwealth and the nation itself. Later today, we will be talking to some of the survivors, when we come back on at 12. Now back to you," Celina said on the TV screen.

"Gun control? Why don't they ever address the

people using them? Mental health is the issue here...well actually, both guns and mental health are at fault here," I said.

"What do you mean?" my dad asked.

"Like, if you can buy a gun anywhere with only a simple background check to see if your clean, that's messed up," I explained. "If you want to lower the rate of gun violence then there needs to be more stringent checks on people who want to buy them, followed by mental health screenings."

"Pete, it's not time to think about that now. You need to concentrate on getting well. School is closed for the rest of year...I wanted you to hear that from me first," he said to me. "All of your friends are out of surgery now. They will be able to leave soon, and so will you," he said.

"Great," I said back.

"I know this is difficult...I told your mother what happened. She knows that you're okay now and out of surgery," he said.

"I hope the government can reach an agreement on this and make laws that connect gun control and mental health," I said.

"Pete...is this really the time to talk about this? I

mean, were the Rossis really insane?" he asked.

"There had to be something wrong with them. Most people wouldn't want to shoot up a school over some election they rigged," I explained.

"True, but we may never know what the real cause was," he said.

"America needs to see a change, and I hope this shooting will open the minds of senators and members of congress. If not, we have to protest, until they do something about it," I said. "What we really need is a stronger background and mandatory mental evaluation before anyone can purchase a weapon."

"The perfect opportunity to bring this issue to the public is when you get an interview with the news later this week. Until then, just relax and wait until the doctor can clear you to go home," my dad told me.

"But we have to do something now!"

"I understand, but it's going to take a long time for America to change."

"They need to know what we went through, they need to see..." I trailed off.

We sat there for awhile, in silence, and I continued to think about everything. I didn't even notice Dr.

Grouse walk into my room, with a clipboard in hand.

"Alright Pete, you are free to go now. Make sure you keep your left arm in that sling for about six weeks so it can fully heal itself, which means no writing with the left hand in that time," he says to me and my dad. "Other than that, you are discharged from here. Take your time leaving if you need to."

"Thanks, Dr. Grouse," Lee said. "Let's go. Pete, get yourself dressed."

My dad gave me some clothes, clean and blood free, a button up orange shirt and green shorts. Today was another warm day, surprisingly, for late November. I got ready and we left the hospital room, making our way out of the building. My dad decided to take my car instead of his, to enjoy the spring-like weather outside.

"I don't know if I can do this," I said.

"Don't worry, I'll go slow," he said.

We drove out of the parking lot and made our way home. No one was waiting for us, but there was plenty of police around. Some neighbors were walking around, others were in cars looking at us or the police. It was early morning on a Wednesday, and Sean, Rudolph, Wilson, Harper, and Ulysses were all home, so I could meet up with them later. Sean was still in some pain, so we all decided to meet up at his house instead of mine. My dad pulled into the driveway and turned off the car. We headed inside of our house to unpack whatever I had with me.

"I don't know what you're going to do for the rest of the day, but I have to go meet with your stepmother and your mother to talk about what happened two days ago," Lee said.

"Alright, the guys and I wanted to meet up at Sean's place to talk. I'll be there if you need me," I said, walking out of the door.

"Okay, be safe out there," he said, waving.

Since we came home from the other way, I couldn't get a look at the Rossi household, but once I was able to, I could see that the police were there. I shook it off and continued to walk to Sean's house. When I was about three houses down, near the infamous bushes were I broke my ribs, I saw Rudolph and Wilson waiting for me.

"Oh hey, I saw you two leaning on the bushes. Were you waiting for me or something?" I asked them.

"We are waiting for Ulysses and Harper to come. They said they would be here by now, but now that you're here, we can go in. Sean's parents left for some reason, but oh well. They might have gone out to run some errands," Wilson said to me.

"We might be here for a long time," Rudolph said.

We made our way into Sean's house, and he was sitting on the couch, watching TV. It was one of those stupid infomercials.

"You're finally here! It has seemed like forever since I've seen you guys. Sit down...my parents aren't home right now," Sean said to all of us.

Sean had a sling on his arm and bandages around his leg and chest, where he was stabbed. Rudolph had bandages wrapped around his chest too. Wilson had a sling, and that was it for him. We all sat down with Sean and got comfortable, while we waited for Ulysses and Harper to stop by.

"We made it...we all survived. I don't know what I would have done, if one of you would have died in that school," Sean said.

"Yeah...same. But the others...who didn't make it..." Wilson stopped, unable to continue.

"What did the first floor even look like, when you were held captive with the other teachers?" Rudolph asked.

"Hell, straight up hell. There was so much blood everywhere, people everywhere, dead and alive," he explained.

"Damn, we were lucky...we never had to go down there and see...we saw the second floor though, the dead bodies," I said.

"Is it true that Ulysses the man killed James and Leo, when they attacked him and Rudolph?" Wilson asked.

"Yes, yes he did as a matter of fact. He didn't want to do it, but he knew he had to save us from death," Rudolph said. "He saved me from getting gutted by Leo's switchblade and Sean and Pete."

Harper and Ulysses walked into the house and took a seat beside me and Rudolph. Ulysses sat close to me, as usual.

"We made it, but not on time of course," Ulysses grumbled loudly.

"Obviously...what took you so long?" I asked.

"Some news crew was trying to interview us, but we kept telling them that we had to go and not to follow us," explained Harper.

"At least, you made it out, all in one piece," Sean said.

Ulysses had a concussion and still had the bandages on his head, after getting discharged from the hospital.

Harper on the other hand had some bandages around his arm and torso, from his stab wounds.

"Whatever happened to Sheriff Ray and Wallace?" I asked.

"They're at the police station now talking with some investigators and FBI agents who came days ago for the voter fraud. The State Police is still out there investigating the crime scene," Ulysses explains.

"The FBI, State police, Sheriff's office, and Local police are still trying to figure out what exactly happened," Harper said.

We all sat and talked about that day, until I got a text from Hazel. She miraculously survived the school shooting because she was sick that day. The award for luckiest person on the planet goes to her for not going to school that day. The text read, *How are you doing? I hope everyone you know is okay.* I respond back with, *Yeah we all made it out. Some of us were shot and stabbed.* She said back, *Did Sean get shot?* I replied, *Yes, he was hurt more than any of all us...almost died.*

I stood up and started to walk to the door to go outside. I still had my phone in my hand as I walked outside, ignoring everyone. I walked to the front of Sean's house and sat on the bench he had in front of a tree. The bench was facing the road, where cars were driving by, not noticing me. There were some police cars but not many.

"Why did you leave us for outside?" Ulysses asked, walking up and sitting beside me.

"It got me thinking…it's only November and school is already canceled for the rest of the year. We lost nearly forty people, mostly students, all over a county-wide election that we just should have stayed out of," I said.

"We did what was right. At least they're dead," Ulysses said.

"You killed two people and saved the three of us. You are totally against violence, but you still saved us," I said.

"If I had to do it again, I would have, anything to save my friends from danger," Ulysses said.

"You are handling things really well," I said.

"You took a .45 caliber in the shoulder like a boss," Ulysses said. "I'm surprised that Sean even survived, taking two with him and being stabbed."

"With all of this death and carnage that happened, it made me think. Why would they even shoot up a high school?" I asked.

"Don't ask that," Ulysses said.

"I'm serious," I said. "And we, the intended targets, all survived while others got murdered for being in the way," I said.

"You can't do that. We were just lucky, being on the top floor instead of at the cafeteria," Ulysses said.

"You still remember a lot, after getting smashed in the head," I said.

"I can forgive, but I can never forget," Ulysses said.

"You and I are usually the first to forgive people, especially Sean at times," I said.

"Yeah, we are sometimes," Ulysses said.

"Alright look, Hazel and I spoke the day before the election, and we talked for a long time. It got a little heated and at other times, weird," I said.

"What did you two talk about?" Ulysses asked.

"We talked about everything really. What was going on with her prior to this event and about you guys and me," I said.

"What did you say…about me?" Ulysses asked.

I froze and just sat there in silence for a few seconds and started to realize that my face was slowly turning red, and I knew Ulysses could see it.

"Well...uh, this is where it started to get weird," I said.

"How so?" Ulysses asked.

"We talked about how you acted around other people in school and the four of us, especially me," I said.

"What do you mean?" Ulysses asked.

"Hazel thinks you're gay," I said.

"No, not at all," Ulysses said.

"See!?! That's what I told her...you're not at all," I said.

"About that, see, listen...I'm not straight either," Ulysses said.

"I know. Hazel and I both agreed that you're bisexual," I said.

"Hazel knows too much for her own good," Ulysses said. "There you go... now you know the truth about me."

Ulysses started to rub his face and laid his hand on his lap and continued to stare at me.

"You don't have to be friends with me if you don't want to, because I'm not normal in your eyes," Ulysses said.

I placed my hand on his leg and looked directly at him, "Don't worry. I'm exactly the same as you. I may be a mental case, according to the doctors, but I can still feel," I said.

"You're joking?," Ulysses questioned.

"No, I'm not joking. Your hair looks... kinda cute," I smiled.

"I've always thought your hair looks cute too," Ulysses laughed.

"I've always thought your eyes were mysterious," I continued.

Ulysses blushed, "So...does that mean you like me?"

I looked away for a moment to think, before meeting his gaze once again, "I do...it's just..." I paused.

"What is it?" Ulysses asked.

"I'm just not sure what I'm... into."

"That's okay. We can figure it out together," Ulysses smiled. "You know," he began, "People at school probably think we've been dating for years because we are so close."

"My parents won't even care I'm with you, really. They always wanted me to be with someone who really cares about me," I rambled.

"My parents won't care either," he paused. "They've probably been expecting it."

We both laughed as we recalled his exceptionally flamboyant tastes. "This means that we can go downtown and sit on some random bench or park and go people watching for a few hours," Ulysses continued.

My smile widened as I watched Ulysses relax. "I was going to hug you, but I forgot about the hole in my shoulder." We both laughed again.

"Maybe, for now, we could just, hold hands."

"That's fine by me," I smiled. With that, he intertwined his fingers with mine. "We should probably go inside," I managed, "before the others think that we left or something."

"Don't worry about it. I told them I was going to talk with you outside and that we would be back whenever we got finished," Ulysses said.

"Alright then," I said.

We sat in silence for a few moments before Ulysses spoke up again.

"When we do go back inside, we should tell them what is going on between us, so that they aren't caught off guard," Ulysses said.

"Yeah, we shouldn't keep it a secret," I affirmed.

We got up and walked over to the house to tell everyone else. Still holding hands, we walked inside to Sean and Rudolph, giving us strange, yet knowing, looks.

"What's happening?" Sean asked.

"We have to tell you three something," I said.

"Okay, what is it?" Rudolph asked mockingly.

"Pete and I are... dating now," Ulysses said.

"Oh, okay. We don't care, we've known you guys for so long, and it is the twenty-first century," Sean said.

"Well, this is good," Wilson said. "It's good to be friends."

Ulysses and I sat beside each other to listen to everyone else.

"We were talking about what we're going to do next, whenever school starts back," Sean said.

"The state has to do something for us in the meantime," Wilson informed us. "The government is slow," I remarked, "We'll be waiting awhile."

"Are you two really a couple, or are you just playing with us?" Rudolph interjected, changing the subject.

"We're serious," I said.

"Prove it then."

"Like how? What are we going to do?" Ulysses asked.

"Kiss or something," Sean said.

"You're just making it awkward now," I said.

"Pete, it will be okay," Ulysses said, turning to face me. I faced him, and his dark green eyes looked right into mine. As he moved closer, I did too, closing my eyes. His lips felt heavy, and a surge of electricity flowed through my body. It was over within a matter of seconds, but it felt like an eternity. I opened my eyes and turned to see everyone staring at us.

"There you go – we're together," Ulysses said.

"Well then, they weren't lying," Sean said.

I stood up and started to walk back outside, and Ulysses followed behind me. "We're heading to Ulysses's house. My parents are home...probably still talking about the shooting. I'll talk with you guys later today," I said to everyone else.

"Have fun," Sean called.

Ulysses closed the door behind us, and as we started down the steps, I felt the cold of his hand fall into mine once again.

24 INTERVIEW

"So, tell me what happened on that frightful day, the 23rd? Try and start from the beginning," the detective said.

"That day was a very dangerous experience. People wouldn't understand what happened that day, not if they weren't there," I said.

I got into my seat next to the detective and started to write out what occurred that day. I started from the beginning of that day and continued until...the shooting started in the cafeteria. I went on, in near perfect detail about the horrific day, so that the sacrifices that were made and the lives that were lost would not be forgotten. And when I got finished, I was allowed to leave the police department with my parents. Once I got home, I started to wonder what the others would say about that day for the police. Ulysses was done before me, so I texted him.

"Pete, it is time for dinner…are you going to come down and eat with us?" Mother gently asked.

"I'll be down in a few minutes…I need to get myself together."

I walked down the steps slowly and went into the kitchen, where my parents were sitting. To my shock, there was also a news reporter, who had been following the story. I had only ever seen her on television. She looked at me and smiled. She was a short lady with dark ginger hair. I thought she had to be crazy.

I wasn't sure what to say. "I thought you were coming over tomorrow."

"I found out about your interview with the police and thought I would stop by. I thought it might be helpful, in case there was anything you wanted to share," she explained.

"What is your name? What station do you work for?"

"My name is Celina, and I work for the Susquehanna news station near Harrisburg, the state capital, and we wanted to get a first-hand experience of that day, to make sure that people hear the real story."

I sat down at the table next to Celina and got my phone out, trying to remember, once again, all that had happened. Part of me had been foolish enough to believe that after the police station, I would be done.

"Let me sit here – I need some time. Please give me a moment with my parents before we start," I stammered.

"Take as much time as you need, Pete; I will wait. Once you share your experience, I'll talk to your friends too. I don't want to rush you, but I want to make sure that all of your voices are heard."

"Thank you," I replied.

Once she left, I just stared at my plate.

"We don't want you to rush," my mom said.

I looked at her, "No, it's okay. I think I am good. I think I need to do this. I'm ready."

I sat down with Celina, and she took out her notebook, trying to look as empathetic as possible.

"You know Pete, I'm glad that you are still keeping positive, after all of the stuff you have been through," Celina said.

I sat down on the couch and tried to gather up my

thoughts. I grabbed my phone from my pocket to open the calendar app and went back in time, to the date that changed everything, and waited for Celina. While I sat there, Sean texted, making me aware that the FBI was going to get involved in the investigation. The magnitude of what I experienced...I just wasn't prepared for it.

"Pete, I'm ready. When you can, please begin," Celina said.

"I'm not sure if it will all seem clear. I know when things started – there was a lot that happened before."

"Time doesn't matter; I have all of the time in the world to listen to your story. Just begin, and I'll get your story," Celina said.

"It started from the middle of November. It began when Ulysses and I started to talk about the new administration election that was supposed to take place earlier last week. Since the year had restarted itself, it was our time for reelection and election. With the admin elections being held also, our election would be a week after theirs so it wouldn't cause and confusion," I explained.

"So you're saying is that you guys wanted to run for reelection and attempt to help out with the new board members that would be taking control in January? Who were the other student members other than you and Ulysses?" Celina asks.

"Since I represent the Red Party as the board leader I had a clerk who was basically my secretary which was Ulysses, Sean was also with the student body as the Historian for everyone, to keep track of everything that we voted on. We are the voting minority with only two voting members Jack and Adam, which means whenever there is a tie I have to break it, which is common. James, Leo, Stefano, and Tom were rest of the Blue Party and held the majority for nearly two years and wanted to knock us out of the seats this year and have a full Blue Party for their last year in school."

"So tell me, what would have happened if they didn't commit voter fraud and shoot up the school, would you guys be able to fend them off in the late November student election?"

"Not a chance, we would have been swiped away in that one, Sean calls it a commie take down of the school, which it really was in a way, they made a case when they were in freshman year of school and everyone liked them, they had somewhat good ideas on how to run a student run government, but their ideology was socialist like, as if they brainwashed the students into liking that kind of stuff, on the other hand, our party represented simple government and wanted all students to have little government in their lives in and out of school, I don't know why they want a government to shove policies down their throats but more power to them I guess."

"Let us say the school wasn't burned to a crisp and school would resume a few weeks after the shooting, who would be in charge?" She asks.

"Since they lost the election, our party would have to take charge with two members and anyone else who ran along the Red Party," I say. "I probably would have retired after this year anyway."

"What about your friends, how did the others who weren't running get involved with the Mafia issue?"

"Since Ulysses and I were running for reelection, the rest were mainly support, Sean was retiring from being the historian, I remember about a week ago everyone but Ulysses and I went on a spying mission to see what the Rossi's were up to, Rudolph said he had witnessed someone go down before Harper got him for our meeting. I told them all to go out and see what's going on there and not to get caught," I tell her.

"What happened when they got back from their investigation?"

"They were all...disturbed I would say, they told us that they had guns and other stuff that would make anyone suspect them of wrongdoing, this mainly followed into the next day and we went to the local cafe and talked about it, I didn't believe them, I just said to myself it was just gear for hunting or self-defense, we live in Pennsylvania after all."

"What do you guy do on Sunday then?"

"We got some stuff for campaigning and that was really it for the most part."

"Monday marked two days before the general election for the county, anything goes down?"

"We came to school as a normal day for the most part until we got to the board meeting that Mr. Mickelson called for on Friday. We were supposed to vote on a repeal on whether or not students would be allowed to eat outside again which was abolished two years before I even came to the school due to fights in school and other issues the staff had to deal with. It was repealed just barely, I had to break the tie, that was the only time I had to go against my own party to pass something and vice versa for them also. But that wasn't the important part of this, I left to use the restroom and was confronted by Hazel, who is part of the Mafia too, she told me that all of the stuff I had been hearing around school and from Sean and the others that they indeed were part of the Mafia and had some evil plans to rig the Mayor and Board election, they didn't have any plans to rig the Sheriff election as he was the only person on that ballot this year."

I pause for a second so Celina could catch up on what I was saying, typing fast on her laptop trying to get every word of importance.

"How did you feel when you were told the real truth of the Mafia organization and their plans to rig the election?"

"At first I thought to myself, Sean was actually right for once, then I realized this was huge and bad, I also wondered why? Ottavio was a community favorite, I even liked him and still have some sympathy for him. Hazel told me that the Mayor and Ottavio conspired together so the Mayor could win his reelection with a deal to help bring 'Mafia influence' deeper into the commonwealth, this is bad because it would have caused high crime, murder, and overall a bad community area, think Chicago, but Mid-Atlantic styled."

"How did you get Sheriff Ray involved in the investigation? How was it so convincing that he had to look into it?"

"After my talk with Hazel I told Sean that he was right first and then told them what Hazel told me, Sean told me about Sheriff Ray somehow he knows Ray. After school Rudolph and I went to Adamstown, to speak with Sheriff Ray, he already knew about a Mafia surprisingly and we just supported his suspicions even more. Get this, McCreedy told Ray to stop investing a possible Mafia years ago because he called it a waste of time and county resources. Which I find extra suspicious, which if you pull some ideas together it shows that Ottavio and McCreedy had an evil plan way before the election cycle. Ray told us he would be at our school the next day to come up with a plan of action against them when voting started Wednesday evening.

"Election time, where were you at during the arrest?"

"When Ray busted down the door, he caught all of them in the action and already had Ottavio arrested, Leo tried to pull a gun on Ray but was quickly subdued by the local police."

"We already know what happened the day after and everything until we lead up to the school shooting on Monday, tell me about Monday before the shooting even started."

"Well, I was in Mr. Mickelson's room which was on the third floor, freshman and sophomores were having lunch as we were in study hall, Harper and Mickelson were downstairs when it all started. The rest of us wanted to find out more about the whole election crisis and we attempted to look it on online, but there was an issue, no signal on the phones and the main phone line at school was cut. People started to walk downstairs to investigate what was happening, we all elected to stay upstairs so we wouldn't get in trouble for leaving our classroom before lunch. Then it started, minutes later we see Harper running from the other side of the building to get us, he opens the door and tells us what is going on. Everyone was white after he said that. We needed to escape the school in order to survive, we left his room and started to make our way to second floor, looking for weapons, we went into the teacher's lounge were the emergency generator was and we turned it on and went to the closest room to press the emergency call button almost all rooms had in it."

"Second floor?"

"The second floor was more dangerous after all, we found Wilson in the bathroom, shot, of course, we continued near the exit until they came to the second floor and found us, shooting at us, hitting Sean and I. We got back to the third floor, Harper blocked off the exit and we tried to hide but they were faster than us getting closer to us on the third floor until Sheriff Ray and Wallace came in from the room saving us in that situation."

"We know from Ray that you guy split up and some stayed upstairs and the others when down to the first floor, what happened during that time?"

"We were taken hostage by Leo and James, they hid in a nearby room, Leo stabbed and knocked out Ulysses and Rudolph were nowhere to be seen. Leo pulls his gun out and forced us to go into a room where he talked to the Sheriff about getting out of here and having us hostage, James couldn't find Ulysses and followed the blood trail to the bathroom. Rudolph came back to the room and started to fight with Leo until Ulysses shot and killed him."

"After that incident what else happened?"

"Negotiations, the release of the hostages, and finally the fire and escape, we left from the top of the building at the helicopter to the hospital."

"There we have it, your story on what happened, I have to interview the rest of your friends and get their side of the story. Anything else you want to add before I go?"

"It's only the beginning of the school year, more issues with come and more people could get hurt, stay vigilant."

"Would you suspect that there could be more organized crime located elsewhere in the United States that we may never know about?"

"Of course, gangs everywhere in America, cities, town, school, and neighborhoods. I wouldn't think they would shoot up a school because they have better things to do other than that. This was just an extremely rare scenario of what could happen if gangs did this. But if they get an idea from this, bad things will happen to the innocent."

"So you're saying that if more gang think it's good to become terroristic America would be under attack by its own citizens?"

"Yes, basically, it's now up to the adults and people in

Washington to deal with, even though we can do something about it but not at a higher degree, it will take time, and time is good and bad."

"If you were ever asked to go on television to speak about you and your friend's experience would you do it?"

"Sure? It can bring exposure and tell people the cold-hearted truth of what we are living in today."

"What about gun control?"

"I...don't really care to say...I rather not support both sides because there will always be someone who doesn't like it, people in Washington can work around it or work together and make a way to have both."

"I think that does it for my interview, I hope you get better and all of your friends, I'll be going to interview the others, everyone will share a different story everything something happens at this big scale."

I stood up and Celina stands up as well, I shake her hand and guide her to the door, saying goodbye in the process. I walk back to the kitchen to see my dad sitting and reading the news on his phone.

"I'm done with my interview, it went well for what I seemed," I said.

"Great, you took some time to speak with her. Your

mother left, I don't know when she's coming back," he said.

"That's fine, she was very nice but strange. She looks like someone who would — you know — be a teacher, short and always wanting to learn more from someone... I guess being a journalist is good enough for her," I said.

"They just want the next big thing and want to be first to it," Dad said.

"She's going over to see Ulysses I think for an interview," I said.

"She's getting around with your friends quiet quickly," Dad said.

"That sounds horrible that way you said it," I said laughing.

"She going door to door to see all of your friends whats what about that?" He said.

"Oh, you were serious," I said.

"No, I'm just messing with you I know what I said," He said.

Reader's Guide School Vendetta

Why that Title?

The Mafia takes matters into their own hands for the people who caught them rigging the election.

How long did it take you to write the book?

It took me three months to complete the book's manuscript from November to late February, around one hundred days. Editing took my editor around two months to do.

What did people think when you told them you were writing a book about a topic that is always controversial?

Most people who I spoke with thought the idea was a

good idea, teachers, and students for that matter, they thought it was a cool idea. The Principle and Head Teacher, were more question filled in why I wrote something of this nature, they didn't find out until I got finished with the Manuscript. I mean they couldn't stop me from writing, but they also thought it was good too, but bad timing in that matter, they just gave good advice in what to do when I got it all complete which helped. Which I wasn't sure, I thought more people would say, writing about a School Shooting is messed up, I guess not where I'm from.

Geography speaking and not time, where does this book take place in real life?

This book takes place in the city of Scranton, Pennsylvania, which is located Northeast near New York, the reason I didn't want it in New York is that it's overused as a Mafia hot spot, but it is still close to New York roots. The population in the book is much lower in real life.

Teachers and Adults?

Sheriff Ray or Weston is based on my History and Geography Teacher at school. Mr. Mickelson is based on a Senator. Mrs. Lurgo is obviously based on the Health Teacher, Dr. Chevalier is based on the building principal at my school. Lastly, Ms. Ray is based on my Algebra Two teacher I had for only one week before I dropped that class for Geometry.

Why Pennsylvania?

Who would suspect a Mafia in Pennsylvania? I wanted it close to New York but not there. Pennsylvania is quiet, an area up north, small towns and cities.

Why have a School Mafia Rig an election?

You don't see a lot of books about a School Mafia, just a regular mafia doing more high stakes stuff in the world, having a simple election rigging would have been their first time doing something that high for their age.

Why have Pete and Ulysses date and not Rudolph who had dyed hair also?

When I was writing this I made a mistake in Chapter 4, where Ulysses stared a little too long at Pete and that is where it ended, this was before editing, I shared it to my Creative Writing and they thought it was a great idea to have Ulysses secretly like Pete. So I tried my best to add that to the book.

What is the School based on?

The School is based on how I would see a school near where I live, but it has an inconvenient floor design in the matter where the second floors stairs are diagonally from the first-floor stairs and in the center is a courtyard with windows facing the inside and out. I have never personally when to that High School so I wouldn't really know how it is laid out.

Joshua Downey an American author and student who resides near Chambersburg, Pennsylvania. He currently goes to High School and is intending on going to college for governmental studies. He also likes to play chess and play games with friends. He anticipates getting his next book out soon.

AUTHOR NOTE

Speaking From The Keyboard

Pete and his friends and the events that happened in this book may be an act of fiction be in the reality of all of this it is true. School is supposed to be a safe place for people to go to in order to get an education and not worry about anything like this to happening to them, this book may be an extremely rare case of a school shooting that consists of more than one killer, but anything in this world is possible. We cannot fail the children in our schools ever. Always remember that the kids today will take control of the world tomorrow and we cannot have a life that could make the world better, be lost so early. Take that into consideration when reading this and watching the news that revolves around schools. People who don't make laws can only do so much for everyone, sometimes that isn't enough and we need help. This is an issue that will stay almost forever and may never go away and there is nothing policy or law can do to stop it, criminals will do whatever they wanted in order to get something, they do not follow the rules. This book does seem unrealistic due to it having a mafia consisting of teenagers with a goal to rig an election for their father or the Godfather to the ones who are not related and shooting a school up because they got caught doing it by a group of students and a County Sheriff. And with that, I hope all of you who had made it this far enjoyed the book.

Synopsis

In Northeastern Pennsylvania, a city in Pikerland County called Dutchville. Pete Mailer, a one with words, and wants to win his re-election as the School Board Leader.

In November the School Board Admins and the President are all up for election along with Sheriff Ray and Dutchville's Mayor, Mr. McCreedy. Pete and his friends and Ulysses go to see Mr. Mickelson for more news about the election and discover that Mr. Rossi is running for board president.

Sean reveals to Pete that Leo and Stefano Rossi have a commie plot to take the School Board with the aid of their dad. While home Harper brings Rudolph and

Rudolph alerts the group about what the Rossi family is doing while at their meeting. Pete orders them to go out on a scout mission leaving Ulysses. When the group returned, terrified, they tell Pete that they are working for organized crime in the hope of rigging the election. Pete doesn't buy it.

During a Student School Board meeting, they bring in Ottavio to speak to the students in what his policies are if elected. Pete goes to the bathroom and confronted by Hazel, Leo's girlfriend, and she rats them out to Pete proving what Sean said on Friday. With this, Pete and Rudolph head out to meet Sheriff Ray. They inform him about the mafia and how they're going to rig the election. The following day Hazel confronts Pete again and why he told the Sheriff.

On election day the group arrives at City Hall and meets with Sheriff Ray. Once positioned Ray takes down Mr. Rossi first, but then the Mayor prevents them from entering the counting room. Once Ray breaks open the door, they arrest the four members in there and the Mayor for conspiracy and voter fraud.

The scandal allows the media to go wild over it and forces school to close until Monday.

On Monday, Pete and Ulysses leave health class and go to Mr. Mickelson's room where Sean and Rudolph are. After noticing the phone signal is down, they see Harper running from the other side of the building. He tells them that Leo, Stefano, James, Thomas, and some associates are shooting people in the cafeteria. While trying to escape they run into Wilson, who tells them they have hostages. Hearing the news, they're attacked by the Mafia causing Pete and Sean to get shot. Sheriff Ray arrives from the roof and spares them from the attack.

Leo and James ambush Pete, Sean. Ulysses wounded and knocked out Ulysses. Holding Sean and Pete hostage, they stab Sean and intimidate the Sheriff. James goes out to finish Ulysses who dragged himself to the bathroom. After hearing gunshots Leo opens the door to see Rudolph, who confronts him getting stabbed in the process, Ulysses comes and shoots Leo.

The school catches fire from the explosives, and they

seize the hostages out by helicopter. After surgery, Pete tells Ulysses that he talked with the Hazel Tuesday night about everyone. The upcoming day Pete goes to the Police Station and produces an official report on what occurred. When he returns, he meets the news journalist who has tracked the situation. She asks for an interview, Pete informs her what lead up to the arrests and the enviable shooting at the school.

SCHOOL VENDETTA

Definitions

M1911: A American made Pistol created by John Brown and adopted by the United States in 1911.

Bisexual: Someone attracted to both sexes.

Zounderkite: A complete idiot who constantly makes clumsy and awkward mistakes.

Wop: An Italian or other southern European. *(Informal Offensive)*

Danke: (German) Thank You